FAIRY TREASURE

Gwyneth Rees

Illustrated by Emily Bannister

First published in 2004 by
Macmillan Children's Books
This Large Print edition published by
BBC Audiobooks by arrangement with
Macmillan Publishers Ltd 2005

ISBN 1 4056 6039 2

British Library Cataloguing in Publication Data available

Printed and bound in Great Britain by
Antony Rowe Ltd., Chippenham, Wiltshire

This book is for the real Ruby, with lots of love

And with thanks to Nathan Hyland, for helping me check out the British Museum

1

Bluebell Hall, where Connie had come to stay for the summer, stood on a hill overlooking a small lake, in the middle of which was an ornamental fountain. A green bank, which was covered in bluebells every spring, sloped down to the lake from the house. Today, in the early morning, three swans were floating next to each other on the water. If Connie had been looking in their direction, she would have seen that each one had a little speck of colour on its back—pinkish red, pale

blue and light green. If she had gone closer she would have seen that the specks of colour were actually fairy dresses, and that each of the three fairies wearing them had delicate fluttery wings that sparkled in the early-morning sunshine.

But Connie wasn't looking. She was carrying a mug of coffee and two slices of peanut butter on toast up to her uncle's study. Normally Aunt Alice made Uncle Maurice's breakfast for him, but today she was too busy writing

2

her latest story. She had asked Connie to make breakfast instead and Connie hadn't minded. At least it gave her something to do. She put everything on a tray, folded a piece of kitchen towel to make a napkin, because she reckoned most people got sticky fingers when they ate peanut butter, and carried it up the stairs, imagining that she was a maid from long ago. It was easy to imagine living in Bluebell Hall, even if, like Connie, you weren't usually into playing pretend games.

She glanced at herself in the hall mirror as she passed. Her mother claimed she had the blue eyes of her Irish great-grandmother, who had entertained Connie's mother and aunt with stories about fairies and leprechauns for hours on end—firmly believing in the little folk herself. Connie had said that she thought her great-grandmother sounded a little bit mad, and her mother had laughed and

3

agreed, but said that she'd had beautiful eyes just the same. Her great-grandmother had had red hair when she was young though, with lots of curls, whereas Connie's hair was black and straight, and right now the ends of it were nearly dangling in Uncle Maurice's peanut butter. If she were a proper maid, she thought, her hair would have to be tucked up neatly inside a little white cap like the ones maids wore in television programmes about olden times.

Connie's aunt and uncle, who never watched television and who were both writers, had rented out a flat for the summer in part of Bluebell Hall—an old stately home. The flat itself was quite small, but the whole house was enormous. Connie hadn't met the old lady who owned it, but she knew she was called Mrs Fitzpatrick, that she didn't have any relatives and that she was too frail to live in the house any more and had moved into a nursing home in the village two months ago. The whole house was now up for sale and Connie's aunt and uncle had to let

prospective buyers view their flat, which didn't please them at all because the reason they had come here for the summer was to get away from other people.

Connie's presence here was another thing they hadn't anticipated, although they had agreed to it because they wanted to help Connie's parents. It had been a last-minute arrangement after the childminder Connie's mother had arranged for the school holidays had cancelled. Both Connie's parents worked and it was impossible for them to take much time off. Obviously Connie couldn't be left at home on her own all day during the holidays and, since Aunt Alice and Uncle Maurice had a spare room in the flat, it was agreed that Connie would stay with them over the summer instead.

'You'll have a lovely time,' Connie's mother had said when Connie had protested at the idea of being sent away. 'The house is in the country and it'll be a holiday for you too.'

'No it won't! Aunt Alice and Uncle Maurice are both *weird*!'

Connie's mother had laughed. Aunt Alice was her sister and she didn't think her weird just a little scatty perhaps. Her brother-in-law, Maurice, *was* a bit eccentric, but he had a good heart and sometimes he could even be quite sociable. The fact that he had jet-black hair that stuck out at all angles and thick black eyebrows that nearly always seemed to be bunched together in a frown made him look a bit scary, that was all.

'Uncle Maurice just *looks* a little different to other people,' Connie's mother had insisted firmly. 'And you know what a mistake it can be to judge somebody by their appearance.'

'Mmm . . .' Connie still wasn't convinced. But since she knew she would have to go and stay with her uncle and aunt in any case, she decided there was no use making a big fuss about it. She knew that her dad's company couldn't do without him over the summer, and neither could the hospital ward where her mum worked as a senior nurse.

When she took in his breakfast,

6

Uncle Maurice was sitting at his computer with his back to her, typing in his thoughts at top speed. Uncle Maurice had told her once that the hard bit about writing was sorting out what you'd put on the page after you'd put it there.  Connie reckoned that if he thought a bit more before he let all those words spill out all over the place then he might not have that problem. Her uncle was always changing what he had written, she noticed. At school, when she had to write a story, she never changed it. If there were any spelling mistakes, her teacher would always pick those up later.

'What's your new book about, Uncle Maurice?' Connie asked him.

'Dragons,' her uncle grunted,

without looking up.

'WOW! Are they good dragons or bad dragons?' Connie supposed that since her uncle was writing a children's book, he would like it if she—a member of his future audience—showed some interest in it. So Connie tried to sound enthusiastic, even though she didn't like reading much at all and, if she ever did read a book, she liked it to be about real children. She didn't really go for stories about things that everyone knew didn't really exist —like dragons and fairies and other make-believe stuff.

'They are both good *and* bad, of course! Like people,' her uncle replied, picking up a piece of toast and biting into it. He was looking at her with his very intense gaze, which used to scare her when she was younger but that didn't any more. Uncle Maurice hardly ever shouted or lost his temper with her, even though he always looked like he was about to. In fact, although Uncle Maurice wrote children's books, he wasn't very comfortable around real children and he freely admitted to

8

finding them quite frightening in large groups. His books had won prizes which Connie supposed must mean they were good, although she hadn't read any of them herself. They were all set in strange worlds or on other planets, and the main characters were always very odd boys who seemed like they had nothing in common with her at all.

Uncle Maurice smiled at Connie. Eating peanut butter always put him in a good mood. 'If you're bored, why don't you go down to the lake?' he suggested. 'There were some fairies down there earlier this morning. They might still be there if you go and look.'

Connie gaped at him in disbelief. *Fairies?* How old did her uncle think she was?

She headed back downstairs feeling fed-up. Perhaps Aunt Alice would come for a walk with her if she asked. Aunt Alice could be quite good company when you got her away from her books. But Aunt Alice—who wrote mainly about children who had adventures in boarding schools—was still busy writing.

Connie sighed. There were no other children here who she could play with and, since there was no television, all she could do here was read. And Connie certainly didn't feel like doing that.

There was one thing she *could* do though. She had noticed the other day that one of the ground-floor windows of the main house had been left open. She had been going to mention it to her aunt, but then decided not to as an idea began to form in her mind. She could climb into the house and go exploring. She wouldn't touch anything or move anything, of course—it would just be fun to see what the rest of Bluebell Hall was like inside.

Connie opened the front door of the flat and went out. The room where the window had been left open was round the other side of the Hall. As she walked across the lawn, she thought what a lovely house this must have been long ago when it was smartly painted and had lots of people living in it. Even though she didn't usually like

10

pretend games, this morning she found herself imagining that she was on her way to join her Mama and Papa in the breakfast room where the servants would be dishing out bacon and eggs from silver platters with shiny lids.

Connie reached the window and found it still open. The curtains were drawn across so she couldn't see inside. The window was the old-fashioned sash kind, where one half slid over the other half when it was opened. A gap had been left at the bottom and Connie pushed the window up until there was a space big enough for her to climb through.

Inside, she found herself in what was obviously a library.

11

After quickly glancing at the wall-to-ceiling shelves of leather-bound books, she tiptoed across the wooden floor towards the door. She wasn't sure why she felt the need to tiptoe when she knew there was nobody else there, but somehow it seemed as if, that way, she would be disturbing the house less than if she walked normally.

Just as she was thinking this, she heard a noise and looked round sharply. The curtain moved and she saw a tiny red fluttery thing fly out from behind it. She blinked. It had to be either a huge red butterfly or a tiny red bird—nothing else made sense—except that it didn't look like either. Before she could get closer to see, something else in the room caught her eye. On a shelf to her right, in amongst all the other large dusty books, was one which was covered in a dust that sparkled.

Connie was moving towards it when there was another noise above her and she looked up to see a huge book hurtling down towards her from the top shelf.

'That was your fault, Emerald!' a cross little voice whispered as Connie sat on the floor, feeling dazed. 'You always get carried away.'

'I do not!'

'Yes, you do! I said to distract her not knock her out!'

Connie hadn't been knocked out, but she had lost her balance when she'd ducked to try and avoid the book, and she'd ended up landing on the floor. She put her hand up to feel her head where the book had hit her. The book itself— which looked like a huge encyclopedia— was lying on the floor beside her.

13

Connie tried to get up, but she couldn't seem to find the energy to stand. Her legs felt paralysed, a bit like in a dream where you wanted to run somewhere but couldn't move your limbs. She couldn't be dreaming though. She knew where she was. She was in the library of the old house.

'Come on, Emerald. We'd better go,' one of the tinkly voices said from above her. 'Ruby, be careful. Don't go too near her.'

'Don't worry, Sapphire. She won't be able to hurt me. She can't even *see* me.'

'She saw you before.'

'She was in the right mind then. Now she's gone back to normal. Look.'

Connie felt a strange fluttery draught just in front of her nose, as if a pair of wings were flapping there. But she couldn't see anything.

Then the room fell completely silent. Connie pulled herself slowly to her feet. She couldn't see where the voices were coming from. Fleetingly, she wondered if she had been knocked out when the book fell on her and she was dreaming after all. She looked

around at the books, trying to spot the one that had been coated in the shimmering dust, but there was no sign of it. She went over to the windows, pulled the velvet curtains back to let in as much light as possible, and turned back to properly inspect the room.

And there in the doorway was a middle-aged couple and a young man in a suit, staring at her.

Connie gulped.

'Who are you?' the young man demanded sharply.

Connie recognized him as the estate agent who had brought some people round to look at the house last week. 'C-Connie,' she stammered.

The man was looking stern. 'You're the girl who's staying with the people in the flat, aren't you? What are you doing in here?'

'N-Nothing,' Connie stuttered, feeling stupid. 'A book fell on me.' She turned to point at the encyclopedia on the floor.

Her mouth fell open and she felt as if she had been hit on the head all

15

over again. The book, which had been there only moments ago, had vanished.

2

'I suppose you thought it would be an adventure to go exploring inside the big house,' Aunt Alice said, when the estate agent had left.

Connie nodded, surprised that her aunt understood without her having to explain.

'Well, it probably wouldn't have been all that exciting,' Aunt Alice continued. 'I shouldn't think there are any secret passages or anything like that. Real life isn't like books, I'm afraid. That's something I discovered myself a long

17

time ago.'

'I wasn't looking for secret passages,' Connie said quietly. 'I was just looking for something to do because I was bored. I'm sorry.

'Bored? Well, I know how to cure that. I can lend you some books to read about some children who go exploring. They're called the Famous Five and—'

'Thanks, but I'm really more of a TV person,' Connie replied.

'Oh . . .' Aunt Alice looked flummoxed, as if she had never heard of anyone liking television more than books before.

'You aren't going to get into trouble with the old lady because of me, are you?' Connie asked quickly. She had been worrying about that ever since she had been caught inside the house.

'Mrs Fitzpatrick? I shouldn't think so. She needs our rent too much, poor thing.'

'Does she?' Connie found that surprising. 'I thought she must be really rich since she owns Bluebell Hall.'

'Her family used to have a lot of money a long time ago. But now all

18

that's left is the house. And Mrs Fitzpatrick needs money to pay the nursing home to look after her, so she has to sell it. Nursing homes are very expensive, you see.' Aunt Alice glanced at her computer screen where her latest story was waiting to be finished. She had been in full flow when the estate agent had arrived with Connie.

'I think I'll go down to the lake and feed the swans,' Connie said, sensing that her aunt wanted to get on with her work. 'Have we got any bread?'

'Of course, darling. Take whatever you want.' As Connie was almost through the door, Aunt Alice added, 'But keep away from the big house, won't you?'

'Yes, Aunt Alice,' Connie mumbled.

She went down to the lake thinking about what had happened just now in the library. She knew what her friend Emma would say if she were there. She would say that the voices Connie had heard had been fairy voices. But Connie didn't believe in fairies.

Connie looked across the water to see the swans gliding towards her. They

19

seemed to have something bright on top of their heads. As they came closer she saw that each one was wearing a crown of red flowers.

'How did you get those?' Connie gasped, staring in amazement at the swans and completely forgetting to offer them any bread.

In answer a cheeky-sounding giggle came from behind her. She turned round quickly to see who it was, but there was nobody there.

*   *   *

The next morning, Connie woke up with a start. She had been dreaming about Emma. Emma had been her best friend since nursery school and they had always been inseparable. Then, just before the summer holidays had started, Emma had moved to Canada to live. Connie could hardly believe her friend was gone and, every time she thought about it, she felt like crying. The worst thing was that Emma had seemed excited about going. She had aunts and uncles and lots of cousins in

Canada and she had been there on holiday. Connie had felt like Emma hadn't really minded leaving her behind at all.

Just before Emma had left, they had had a silly argument because Emma said she had lent Connie a book that she wanted back. Connie was sure she had given the book back to Emma ages ago.

In the dream, Connie had taken Emma into the library of the old house and they had found the missing book. Then they had opened it up and lots of bright sparks had started jumping out of it, fizzing like sparklers on bonfire night—except these ones weren't on the ends of sticks but in the air, whizzing around. Emma was laughing happily as she turned to Connie and said, 'They're fairies, Connie. Look! I told you fairies were real!'

That was the moment Connie had woken up.

Connie looked at her bedside clock. It was ten past seven. She knew that her aunt was probably still asleep and her uncle was probably already in his

21

study writing, since he tended to start work very early. She quickly got dressed, opened her bedroom door and crept outside.

Connie was a practical child by nature—not a particularly imaginative one. She had never believed before that her dolls could come to life at night and throw tea-parties (as Aunt Alice had once tried to tell her when she was little) or that there was any such thing as fairies (as Emma had often tried to convince her). But the dream had left her with a funny feeling. She felt as if, all of a sudden, she wasn't so certain about everything any more. And she really wanted to go back to the library.

The library window had been shut and locked by the estate agent— Connie had seen him do it herself—but now it was open again, so she climbed in.

The curtains were still closed so the room should have been dark inside, but it wasn't. It was lit up with dancing specks of light, as if a mirror ball were hanging from the ceiling.

Connie could hear a small, tinkly voice singing: 'Dust, dust, go away! Come back another day!' And high up on one of the shelves she could see something red moving about. For a moment she wondered if she were still in bed, still dreaming, then the little voice called out, 'Ah! You can see me now! Good! Hang on! I'm coming down!'

And suddenly, flying right in front of Connie's face, was a tiny fairy-girl.

Connie gasped and stepped backwards.

The fairy had a smiling face with long red hair tied back with a ruby-red star-clasp. Her dress was a pinkish-red colour and seemed to make a rustling sound as she flew. When Connie looked more closely, she saw that it was made of crêpe paper that had been cut in a spiky way at the hem. Under the skirt was a petticoat made from several layers of delicate tissue paper. She had shimmery wings that flapped behind her, and she was holding something in

23

her hand that Connie at first thought was a fairy wand, but then saw was a tiny feather duster.

'Hello,' the fairy said, cheerfully. 'I'm Ruby. Who are *you*?'

'C-C-Connie,' Connie spluttered.

Ruby giggled. 'That's a funny name, C-c-connie.'

'It's *Connie*,' she managed to say, without stammering this time.

'That's a funny name too!'

Connie was about to argue that it wasn't—and that she liked her name—but it seemed ridiculous to start arguing with a fairy. After all, she could still hardly believe she was really seeing one.

'Ruby is a nice name, don't you think?' the fairy continued. 'I'm called it because of my red hair and because, when I wear red, I sparkle like a red jewel—at least I used to at home. *Everything* sparkles where I come from—even the dust!' The fairy broke off, looking less cheerful. 'Of course, I'm stuck here now. Nothing much sparkles here.' She looked down at her yellow feather duster and sighed.

24

Connie looked round the room. There had to be hundreds of books here and none of them looked like they had been dusted in a very long time. 'What are you doing here?' she asked. 'And how did you get stuck?'

'My job is to rearrange these books,' Ruby said. 'I have to sort them into categories to make it easier for people to find the book they want. I'm arranging them in order of excitingness. I've already designed the labels. Do you want to see?' Before Connie could answer, she had flown up to the shelf above her and was pulling out a piece of paper from behind the row of books.

She let go of it and it fluttered down into Connie's hand. On the paper Ruby had printed the following four headings:

1) *Unputdownable,*
2) *A pretty good read,*
3) *OK—but you won't want to read this all in one go,*
4) *This book makes you fall asleep.*

'Of course, I've got to read them all first before I can divide them up,' Ruby added.

'But that'll take you ages!'

'I know, but I have to do a good deed for humans to make up for something else I did that was bad,' Ruby said, flushing slightly. 'I didn't mean to do the bad thing, but I did—so the fairy queen says I have to make up for it by sorting out this library for any humans who might come here in the future.'

Connie wanted to ask what the bad thing had been, but she didn't quite dare. Not yet. She gave the sheet of paper back to Ruby and sat down on the rug with her legs crossed. 'I still can't get my head round this!'

Ruby sat on the floor beside her, folding back her wings. 'Round what?'

'Round the fact that I'm seeing *you*! That I'm talking to a real *fairy*!'

'It's not so strange. You're in the right mind to see me now. You weren't the other day—at least not for very long. That's why you couldn't see me after Emerald dropped that book on

26

your head.'

'What happened to the book?' Connie asked. It seemed to just disappear.'

'I lifted it back on to its shelf when you were opening the curtains. I used some fairy dust. It practically flew back up by itself—all I had to do was give it a prod in the right direction. Emerald didn't mean to hurt you, by the way. She just wanted to distract you. We're not meant to let humans see the—' She broke off abruptly. 'See *us*, I mean. Especially not ones like you.'

'How do you mean? Ones like me?'

'Ones who don't believe in fairies. They're the ones you have to watch out for. They get such a fright when they actually have a lapse and see us, that they act in very unpredictable ways. It can be most unpleasant.'

'But *I* would never hurt you,' Connie protested. 'You don't need to be afraid of me.'

'I know, but Emerald is very jumpy. An old lady threw a saucepan of tomato soup at her once and it's made her very nervous around humans ever

27

since. That's why she panicked.'

Connie looked around the room, suddenly wondering if jumpy Emerald was hiding somewhere right now, getting ready to launch another book in her direction. 'Where are the other fairies today?' she asked.

'At home in fairyland. That's where I used to live too. But now I have to live here and I can't go home until I finish sorting out all these books—or until I make right the wrong thing that I did.'

Now Connie couldn't stop herself asking. 'What *was* the wrong thing that you did?'

But Ruby shook her head and looked away. 'You might not like me if I tell you and then you won't come to see me again. It gets so lonely stuck here on my own. Emerald and Sapphire are only allowed to visit me once a week.'

'Of course I'll come and see you again!' Connie protested. 'I'm lonely here too.'

'Are you?' Ruby looked surprised. 'Haven't you got any friends here either?'

28

No.' Connie swallowed. 'I had a best friend, Emma, back at home, but she moved to Canada with her family last month. She's the same age as me well, she will be next week when she has her ninth birthday.' Connie felt her eyes filling up with tears as she thought of her friend enjoying her birthday without her. 'I was going to give her a really special present before she left, but we fell out about something really silly and I thought she didn't care about leaving me any more, so I didn't buy her anything. I was wrong though. I really wish I'd got her something now.'

Ruby didn't speak, but watched as a big tear spilled out on to Connie's cheek. 'Don't,' she ordered, as Connie reached up to brush it away. Then Ruby flew up until she was level with the tear, leaned forward and kissed it gently. 'Now catch it in your hand,' she said.

Connie put up her hand to catch the teardrop as it rolled off her chin, and saw straight away that it was glittering. 'Wow!' she gasped.

'Keep hold of it,' Ruby instructed,

reaching inside a pocket in her dress and pulling out a little gold case. Inside the case was a tiny needle and golden thread. As Connie watched, Ruby pushed the needle and thread through the teardrop and out the other side so that now the tear was attached to the thread like a pendant on a gold chain. 'You can send her this if you like—a sparkly teardrop necklace especially for her.'

'Oh . . .' Connie began, but she couldn't find any words to thank her new friend.

'You'd better go now,' Ruby said, briskly. 'I need to get on with some reading. Tell Emma that this necklace will always sparkle so long as it's worn by a person who believes in fairies.'

Connie promised that she would come and visit again tomorrow, as Ruby flew up towards the top shelf and disappeared behind some books. When Connie looked down again at her outstretched palm, the necklace was still there and the teardrop was still sparkling.

3

When she got back, Connie found her aunt putting down the phone. 'Oh, there you are, Connie. I thought you were still in bed. That was your mother. She's going to phone you this evening. That was just a quick call to remind me it's my wedding anniversary today. I forgot all about it, but your mother's right—your uncle and I were married fifteen years ago today. I think I might make a special meal tonight to surprise Uncle Maurice. What do you think?'

'That's a great idea!' Connie replied. 'What are you going to make?'

'Oh dear, now that's the thing.' Aunt Alice frowned. 'If I make a special meal I'll have to do a lot of cooking, won't I?' Aunt Alice rarely cooked proper meals because she didn't like to waste her creative energy on anything other than writing. Since Connie had arrived, they'd eaten either tinned soup, things on toast or ready meals that only had to be heated up in the oven. Connie didn't mind because there was always plenty of biscuits and stuff to munch in between meals so she was never hungry. (Aunt Alice had a sweet tooth and liked to nibble when she was writing because she said it helped her to concentrate.)

'I could help you,' Connie said. 'We can make something easy and walk to the village together to get the ingredients. It'll be fun! And then I can post the birthday present I've got for Emma.'

Aunt Alice saw the excited look on Connie's face and decided she couldn't say no, even though she didn't much

feel like a long walk to the village. 'I suppose I could take a break from my writing today . . .' She smiled at her niece. 'Go and tell Uncle Maurice we're going to the shops. Ask him if he wants us to bring anything back for him.'

Five minutes later, Connie raced back downstairs again, clutching her purse and the necklace, which she had wrapped carefully in tissue and slipped inside the birthday card she had already chosen for Emma. 'He wants some jelly babies,' she said. 'He says the dragon in his book has been eating them all morning and it's given him a craving for them.' She raised her eyebrows to show that she thought her uncle was totally mad, and Aunt Alice laughed as she led the way out the front door.

Connie had forgotten just how much fun Aunt Alice could be when she wasn't writing. On the way to the village they chatted about all sorts of things and played *I Spy* and looked at all the wild flowers, trying to guess their names. Aunt Alice told her all

about the games she had played with Connie's mother as a child.

'Though we didn't always play together,' she added. 'I was always a bookish type and she was always the sporty one. Oh yes, your mother was much more of an outdoor girl than me.'

Connie thought about that. 'I think I'm more of an outdoor girl too,' she said. 'At least I was until—' She just stopped herself from saying, 'Until I met Ruby.'

In the village they went to the post office and Connie bought a padded envelope to put her card and present for Emma inside. Then she copied out Emma's new address on the front and paid for it to be sent to Canada. The lady said that it should be there in time for Emma's birthday next week. After that, they went to the butcher and the greengrocer and bought the ingredients to make a shepherd's pie for dinner, and then they went to the little old-fashioned sweet shop to get Uncle Maurice's jelly babies. The sweets were stored in big plastic jars on

34

the shelves behind the counter and, when they asked for the jelly babies, they had to be weighed out. Connie asked for some chocolate raisins too. While they were waiting, Connie spotted something else on the counter. It was a little pink tube and on the outside it said FAIRY DUST SHERBET.

'I'll have one of those too, please,' Connie said, thinking that it was the perfect gift for Ruby.

They left the shop and Aunt Alice suggested that they went to the little teashop in the village for lunch. Connie had a cheese and ham toastie from the lunch menu and an ice cream afterwards, and Aunt Alice, having a sweet tooth, ordered the cream tea for two for herself. They were both pleasantly full when they walked home together and Connie felt like this was the best time she'd had with her aunt since she'd arrived. And as she had also found out today that fairies were real, she reckoned this had to be one of the best days in her whole life.

*　　　*　　　*

When Connie's mother phoned that evening, Connie was feeling so excited about meeting Ruby that she nearly told her mum about it. But before she could, her mother told her that a postcard had arrived that morning from Emma and she started to read it out to her over the phone.

> *Dear Connie* (her mum read),
> *I hope you are OK and having a good school holiday. I really like Canada and there is a girl my age who lives next door, and guess what? She's called Connie too! I hope that we are going to be really good friends. I am having a birthday party next week. All my cousins are coming and so is Connie. Write soon! Love from Emma*

After that, Connie felt less excited. For the rest of the evening she couldn't

36

stop thinking about that card—and the other Connie who was going to Emma's birthday party instead of her. That night she found that she couldn't sleep.

Her aunt and uncle had gone to bed too and the house was in darkness. She got up and put on her dressing gown and slippers, then crept out of her room, picking up the paper bag of sweets on the way. The front door creaked a bit as she opened it, but it didn't seem as if anyone had heard. The moonlight was strong enough to light her path as she crept round to the main part of the house. She paused to look at the grassy bank that sloped down to the lake. The whole bank seemed to be sparkling, but it could have just been the way the moon was shining on it.

'Ruby!' she whispered, poking her head inside the open library window. 'Are you there?'

'Come in!' a laughing voice said.

As soon as she climbed inside, a set of fairy lights was switched on and Ruby flew forward to greet her saying,

37

'I found these in one of the attic rooms. What do you think?'

'Very pretty,' said Connie. 'Here. I've brought you a present.' She pulled out the sherbet fairy dust and gave it to Ruby. At the same time a chocolate raisin fell out of the bag, and it was that which made Ruby shriek with delight.

'Chocolate! You've got chocolate! Oh, please can I have some?' She quickly explained that chocolate was something that all fairies loved, but which you couldn't get in fairyland. 'It must be wonderful being a human and getting to eat chocolate all day!'

'We don't eat it *all* day,' Connie laughed.

'I would if *I* were a human!' Ruby was almost drooling now, in a very unfairy-like way, as she hovered over the top of the bag.

'You can have them as well as the sherbet if you like,' Connie said. 'But don't eat them all at once or you might get sick.' She wondered as she spoke if it was actually possible for a fairy to be sick.

'Oh, Connie, you're my best friend

ever!' Ruby gushed, diving headfirst into the bag and pulling out a chocolate-coated raisin that filled both her hands.

After they had sat together for a little while, munching the sweets, Connie told Ruby about Emma's postcard.

'She's got a new best friend now who's even got the same *name* as me. Emma won't miss me now she's got *her*, will she? She'll probably forget all about me.'

Ruby stopped licking the chocolate shell of her raisin. 'Will something bad happen to you if she forgets about you? Will you get sick or die or disappear or something?'

'Nothing will *happen* to me,' Connie said, impatiently. 'But—'

'That's OK then,' Ruby interrupted, sounding hugely relieved. She went back to licking at her chocolate.

'No, it's NOT OK!' Connie snapped, feeling her bottom lip start to tremble.

Ruby looked up again in surprise.

'I'm sorry. I just meant . . .' She broke off, frowning. 'Look, let's just forget about that friend of yours. We'll never talk about her again, OK?'

Connie shook her head, speechlessly. She couldn't quite make sense of her feelings about Emma at the moment but she did know that, even though she was angry with her, she didn't want to forget about her.

'Connie, why don't you be *my* best friend, instead?' Ruby asked, before Connie had time to speak.

Connie sniffed. 'Well . . .'

'Good because, if you're my best friend, I can ask you to help me with something.'

'What?' Connie rubbed her eyes with her sleeve.

'I need you to help me make right the bad thing that I did. Will you? Will you help me, so I can go home again?'

Connie narrowed her eyes slightly. 'You haven't told me what the bad thing *was* yet.'

Ruby took a deep breath. 'I will, I promise, but first I have to explain a bit more about us—fairies, I mean. You

40

see, there are different types of fairy. There are flower fairies—they're the most common—and there are other types too. I am a book fairy.'

'A *book* fairy?'

'That's right. The way my world links up with your world is through certain magic books in libraries called entry-books. You can tell an entry-book from an ordinary book because it's covered in fairy dust that sparkles when the book is being used. Only people who believe in fairies can see it sparkling, of course.'

Connie immediately remembered seeing the book covered in sparkling dust on the first day she had gone to the library. She started to look around the room, trying to spot it again, but she couldn't.

'We can fly in and out of your world through those books, you see,' Ruby continued. 'That means we can visit any part of the human world we want— so long as there's a library there with an entry-book in it.' She paused, as if the next bit of the story wasn't so easy to relate.

41

'Sapphire and Emerald and I found *this* library and, when we found we could get out through the window to the lake and go riding on the swans, we came here whenever we could. But one day I came here on my own.' Ruby frowned. 'I was exploring upstairs. The old lady still lived here then, so I had to keep out of her way—I had a feeling she might be the type to believe in fairies, which meant she'd be able to see me. I was having a look in her bedroom and I found some treasure. It was inside an old silver box. I'd never seen real human treasure before, but I'd read about it in books so I was really excited. I wanted to try some on just to see what I'd look like wearing it. Most of the treasures were too big for me, but then I found the ruby ring.'

'It sounds like what you found was Mrs Fitzpatrick's jewellery box,' Connie said.

'The treasure *was* mostly jewels,' Ruby agreed, 'and this ring had little rubies all around one half of it, and it was the right size to fit on my head like a crown. I looked so pretty wearing it. I

42

really wanted to show the others, but Sapphire and Emerald hadn't come with me because they were too busy getting ready for the fairy party we were having that night. Then I thought, why don't I wear the ruby crown to the party? I can borrow it for one night, then bring it straight back. I was so excited that I forgot the rule—' She broke off, looking ashamed.

'What rule?' Connie asked.

'The fairy rule that says that when fairies pass from *your* world into *our* world, they can't take anything with them that doesn't come of its own free will. You see, I forgot to ask the ring if it wanted to come.'

'How can you *ask* a ring something? A ring is just a thing—it can't talk.'

'Things know where they want to be, just the same. If a fairy asks something if it wants to come with her into fairyland and the thing starts to glow like it's covered in fairy dust, then that's a sign that it's saying yes. Sapphire and I took an injured toy soldier back with us into fairyland soon after we first came here. It wanted to

come with us because it didn't like being left upstairs in the old nursery all by itself. And once I took a bookmark that had fallen out of someone's book in a library and was getting all dirty because it had been put in the rubbish bin. It was desperate to come with me. But you see, that ring must have not wanted to come—some things don't—so when I tried to take it through into our world, it vanished.'

'Vanished?' Connie stared at Ruby. 'Into nothing, you mean?'

'No—it just went somewhere else. The fairy queen says things always go to the location of their happiest moment here on earth. I thought the ring might have had its happiest moment here in this house, but I looked everywhere and I couldn't find it. I heard the old lady tell her housekeeper that it had been in her family for generations. I listened very hard to see if the old lady would say any more about it, but she didn't. Then she started to think her housekeeper's son might have stolen the ring when he came to visit his mother and the

44

housekeeper got upset and left and never came back. Then, when the old lady was trying to climb the stairs on her own one day, she had a fall and broke her hip and she couldn't stay in the house alone afterwards. She ended up having to move into that nursing home in the village. She got her lawyer to organize a search of the house to try and find the ring, but it was no good. He couldn't find it either. And unless *I* find it and give it back, I can't go back to my own world—not for ages anyway. Not until I've read and sorted out every one of these books.' Ruby finished speaking and looked at Connie. 'The fairy queen says that fairies who cause trouble for humans have to be punished. But I didn't mean to cause any trouble, Connie. I honestly didn't mean to.'

Connie looked thoughtful. 'I don't think you're a bad fairy,' she said, slowly. 'Perhaps you just didn't *think* enough about what might happen before you did what you did. Something like that happened to me once. When I was little, I wore one of

45

my mum's necklaces to school without asking her. I must have not done the clasp up properly and it came off. We couldn't find it anywhere. I felt terrible because it was my mum's favourite necklace and she was really upset. So, even though I didn't mean to hurt my mum, I hurt her quite a lot.' Connie flushed as she remembered.

'I wish fairies could use their magic to turn back the clock and change things sometimes,' Ruby muttered softly. 'But it's not allowed.'

Connie frowned. 'I'd *like* to help you, but the thing is—I'm not sure *how* to. I mean, I don't know where Mrs Fitzpatrick's ring had its happiest moment, any more than you do.'

'You can go and see her and, ask her though, can't you? She probably knows lots about what happened to that ring in the past.'

'But I don't know her,' Connie protested. 'She might not want me to go and see her.'

'Why don't you take her some flowers from her garden?' Ruby said, flying over to the window to look out.

46

'Then you'll have a good reason to visit.'

'There aren't any flowers in the garden,' Connie said, yawning. It was true. The house's flower beds hadn't been looked after in a long time and they were mostly full of weeds.

'I sprinkled some fairy dust on the bank earlier this evening. Come and look.'

Connie went over to the window. Outside the house the moonlight was shining down on the lake and the garden, and Connie couldn't believe her eyes when she saw what was out there. 'WOW!' she gasped.

The grassy bank outside—which she had thought looked strangely sparkly earlier on—was now totally covered in purple bluebells.

47

4

'This is ridiculous!' snorted Uncle Maurice after he had opened his post the following morning. 'Look at this, Connie! Does that look like the fiercest dragon in the universe to you?'

The first illustration for the front cover of Uncle Maurice's new book had just been sent to him from his publisher. Apparently, front covers needed to be ready a very long time before the publication day of the book—which explained why the people who published Uncle Maurice's books

had already started work on the cover, even though the book itself wasn't even finished.

Connie looked at the picture and smiled. 'The dragon does look quite *friendly*,' she agreed.

Aunt Alice came over to look too. 'I expect they didn't want to put childen off by making him too scary,' she said. Aunt Alice didn't really approve of writing scary stories for children.

'Nonsense!' Connie's uncle burst out. 'Children *love* scary stories. The scarier the better! And this is a story about a *scary* dragon, not one who looks like a great big pussy cat!'

'It's not very scary to eat jelly babies,' Connie pointed out. 'Maybe you should make him eat real babies instead.'

Her uncle glared at her. 'I shall phone them right now and tell them what I think of this,' he snapped. 'And then I'm going to add a few things myself to this picture—bigger nostrils for one thing! Then I'll go down to the post office and send it straight back to them.'

'If you're going to the village,' Connie put in, quickly, 'can I come with you? I've picked some flowers and I'd like to take them to Mrs Fitzpatrick.'

Uncle Maurice just grunted and left the room, but Aunt Alice looked across at her and smiled. 'What a lovely idea, Connie. Where did you find some flowers? I haven't seen any in the garden.'

'There are some bluebells on the bank,' Connie said, flushing slightly. 'I picked some yesterday.'

'Bluebells? At this time of year? Are you sure they're bluebells, Connie? Let me see.'

So Connie went to fetch the big bunch of flowers she had picked last night and put in a bucket of water in her bedroom.

Her aunt looked surprised when she saw them. 'You're quite right, darling. They are bluebells. How odd. They must be fairy flowers then.'

'*What?*'

'Fairy flowers was the name my grandmother used to give to flowers

50

that bloomed out of season. She said it
meant that the fairies had been at
work.'

'Was that your Irish grandmother?
The one who believed fairies were
real?'

'That's right. She was always trying
to get your mum and me to believe that
too.'

'And *did* you?'

'Only when we were very little—
much younger than you are now.' Aunt
Alice smiled. 'I think fairies are a
lovely *idea*, especially for children. Of
course, your uncle thinks they're more
than just an idea—but then he thinks
differently to me about a lot of things.'

Connie remembered how her uncle
had told her there were fairies down by
the lake. She had thought he was only
teasing her.

Later that morning, as she sat in the
passenger seat of her uncle's car on the
way to the village, Connie sneaked a
look at him. It was hard to imagine him
believing in fairies, even if he did write
stories about dragons. 'Aunt Alice says
she doesn't think fairies are real,' she

began, cautiously. 'But that you do.' She waited to see if her uncle would deny it.

'Don't start me on that topic,' Uncle Maurice replied, sounding gruff.

'What? Fairies?'

'Believing and not believing. You don't hear people going around asking each other if they believe in children, do you? Or dogs? Or anything else that's plainly there, right under their nose.'

'Do you think fairies are there, right under people's noses then?' Connie asked, staring in surprise at her uncle.

'Course they are! Most people are just too positive to see them, that's all.'

'Too *positive?*' Connie felt confused.

'That's right. Too positive that there's no such thing. No wonder they never see them, if that's the way they think, eh? It's doubtful people who see fairies, Connie—not ones who think they know everything there is to know.'

They had just reached the nursing home, which was situated on the edge of the village. 'Here you are. I'll come and fetch you when I'm done at the post office,' Uncle Maurice said.

Connie was left to walk up to the front door of the old people's home alone, still thinking about what her uncle had said. Could it be a *good* thing to be doubtful then? She had always thought that being doubtful was something to be avoided. She rang the bell and waited. Eventually the door was opened by a young woman in a white nurse's dress and a blue cardigan.

'I've come to visit Mrs Fitzpatrick,' Connie said.

The nurse looked at the flowers and smiled at her. 'Well, that's a nice surprise for her. She's sitting in the garden. I'll take you through.' As they walked along the hallway she asked if Connie was a relative of the old lady.

'No, but I'm staying in her house. These are from her garden,' Connie added.

'Bluebells still growing at this time of year? That's unusual, isn't it?'

'My auntie says they must be fairy flowers,' Connie said.

The nurse laughed.

Mrs Fitzpatrick was sitting in a

wheelchair next to a table at the top end of the garden. She was reading a book with large print. She took off her glasses as the nurse crouched down beside her.

'Mrs Fitzpatrick, you've got a visitor. And look what she's brought you.'

'I'm Connie,' Connie said quickly. 'I'm staying in your flat at Bluebell Hall with my aunt and uncle. These flowers are from your garden.'

The nurse left them together. Mrs Fitzpatrick's grey-blue eyes narrowed as she stared first at Connie then at the flowers, then back at Connie's face again. She had white hair set in neat curls, and a very wrinkled face that had a bit too much face powder on it.

'What month is it?' Mrs Fitzpatrick demanded. She had a strong voice for such a frail-looking old lady.

'July.'

'Well, the bluebells at the Hall should be over by now—May is their time.'

'I know, but these must be special ones, I think.'

Mrs Fitzpatrick put out her hand to take the flowers. Her hands were very shaky, but they seemed to steady themselves once she had the bunch of flowers in her grasp. 'Beautiful,' she pronounced. As she looked at Connie, her eyes seemed to lose their greyness and become almost the same shade of purply-blue as the flowers.

'Shall I ask the nurse to put them in a vase for you?' Connie offered.

'Later.' Mrs Fitzpatrick held them to her nose and sniffed them. 'Lovely. Tell me your name again.'

'Connie. I thought the bluebells might remind you of your home. In case you were missing it.'

'I don't miss it,' the old lady grunted. 'Not how it is now anyway. I only miss how it used to be when I was a girl—that's the Bluebell Hall I like to

remember.'

'I think I miss it how it used to be too,' Connie said. Then she blushed because she realized how silly that sounded. 'What I mean is that I've been trying to imagine how it must have looked before it . . . well, when it was all grand and lovely . . and I'm really sorry that I never got to see it when it was like that.'

Mrs Fitzpatrick nodded as if she understood. 'It was very impressive when I was young. Full of people. Not like now. My parents always had lots of friends. They used to throw big parties at the Hall. My sister and I used to watch all the guests arriving from the upstairs landing. The entrance hall was always my favourite part of the house. You should go inside and have a look sometime.'

Connie suddenly felt the urge to confess. 'I hope you don't mind, but your library window was open and I climbed through to look inside. I know I shouldn't have without asking and I'm sorry. Your estate agent caught me and he was very cross.' She frowned. 'Did

he tell you?'

The old lady shook her head, not looking too concerned. 'Nobody tells me anything these days. Nobody wants to worry me. That lawyer of mine thinks I worry very easily just because I'm old, but he's mistaken. I was never the worrying kind. Took after my father in that way. That's why he and I got on so well. Used to drive my poor mother mad with the things we'd get up to that made *her* worry.' Mrs Fitzpatrick laughed.

Connie took a deep breath. Since they seemed to be talking about the past . . .

'There's something I wanted to ask you,' she began, feeling her face grow hot. 'Have you found your ruby ring yet?'

Mrs Fitzpatrick looked surprised. 'How do *you* know about that?'

Connie inwardly kicked herself. What could she say now? She could hardly say that she knew about it because a fairy had told her. But before she could say anything at all, Mrs Fitzpatrick continued talking.

57

'Of course, everybody knows everything in this village. I expect my housekeeper told everyone *she* knew and they told everyone *they* knew and now I don't suppose I can expect it to be news to anyone. No, my dear. I haven't found the ring.' She sighed. 'It's been in my family for six generations, you know. I didn't have any children or I would have passed it on to them. I was going to leave it to my niece in my will.'

'It must be really old,' Connie said. 'Do you know who gave it to your family in the first place?'

'Interested in history, are you?' The old lady smiled. 'Nice to find a young person who is for a change. The ring was first given to one of my ancestors about two hundred years ago, I think. One of the daughters of the house was in love with a young man of a neighbouring family. He gave her the ring as a parting gift just before he went off to fight in a war. He was killed in battle and the story is that she planted a tree in memory of him at the spot where he'd given her the ring—

58

the place in the grounds of Bluebell Hall where they always used to meet.'

Connie felt excited. 'Whereabouts was that? Is the tree still there?'

'Oh yes. It's a very tall oak tree now, just inside the grounds of the house, at the very back where our family's land used to meet the land of our neighbour.'

'Is the oak tree easy to find?' Connie asked.

'It's the only oak tree there—the wishing tree, my sister and I used to call it.'

Just then, the nurse came back, carrying a tray of tea and biscuits. She took the flowers away with her to put them in a vase.

'Well, Connie, it's very nice of you to come and see me. I don't get many visitors these days. Make sure you never run out of friends the way I have, my dear. It can be very lonely if you do.

'Sometimes your friends run out on *you*,' Connie pointed out, thinking about Emma.

Mrs Fitzpatrick nodded. 'That's true! Mine have nearly all died on me

59

over the past ten years. Very inconsiderate of them!' She smiled wryly. 'The good thing about coming to live here is that it gives me the chance to make some new ones. At least that's the idea. I've been getting on pretty well with Hester over there.' She pointed to an old lady sitting on her own in the shade, knitting. 'She likes to keep herself to herself a lot of the time, like me, but in the evenings she's always ready for a game of Scrabble.'

When the nurse returned soon afterwards, with the bluebells neatly arranged in a big blue vase, Uncle Maurice was with her.

'Hi, Uncle Maurice!' Connie greeted him.

Mrs Fitzpatrick looked up and didn't bother to hide her astonishment when she saw Uncle Maurice's eyebrows. 'Good grief!'

'Good morning,' Uncle Maurice replied, ignoring Mrs Fitzpatrick's gaze as he grunted at Connie. 'Ready?'

Connie nodded.

Uncle Maurice reluctantly shifted his eyes over to the old lady and asked,

awkwardly, 'How are you then? All right?'

Connie thought that her uncle's manners could do with a bit of brushing up—but then so could Mrs Fitzpatrick's.

'I am very well, thank you. And since you're here, I may as well inform you that Bluebell Hall has been sold and that you will therefore have to vacate the flat by September at the latest. That's when the new people want to take possession.'

'The house is sold?' Connie gasped. 'Who to?'

'A couple who went to see it the other day. They want to turn it into a country health club apparently.'

'But what about all your things? What about the library?' Connie asked, thinking of Ruby.

'There'll be an auction. Everything will have to go. The books too.' Mrs Fitzpatrick sighed wistfully. 'Those books were my father's pride and joy.'

Connie nearly cried out, *But you can't get rid of the library! Ruby hasn't finished sorting out the books yet!* But

she just managed to stop herself. After all, if they found the ring then Ruby could go back home again straight away in any case. And now that Connie thought she knew where the ring had had its happiest moment, all she and Ruby had to do was find the oak tree that marked that spot in the grounds of Bluebell Hall.

5

'I'm so excited,' Ruby said, as she and Connie set off across the rough grass behind the house, towards the old oak tree.

It was quite a trek through long grass—the grounds of Bluebell Hall were huge—and Connie wasn't able to go as fast as Ruby, who soon started to complain that her wings were getting tired from having to fly so slowly.

'Go on ahead if you want,' Connie said. 'I'll meet you at the tree.'

'I won't be able to tell which one it

63

is. I don't know what an oak tree looks like.'

'I thought fairies *knew* things like that.'

'Flower fairies do—they're crazy about nature and all that outdoor stuff—but we book fairies have always got our heads stuck in a book, so we don't know so much about plants and flowers and things.'

The two of them carried on together. After a while Ruby rested on Connie's shoulder, which was no problem for Connie, since fairies don't weigh anything.

Eventually they came to the tree that Mrs Fitzpatrick had described.

'Imagine . . .' murmured Connie. 'Two hundred years ago, that man and lady met at this spot and he gave her the ruby ring.'

Ruby didn't reply. She was too busy flying round the trunk of the tree, looking for places where a ring could be hiding.

'I'll look at the bottom of the tree,' Connie said. 'You'd better fly up and start looking in its branches.'

They hunted high and low all afternoon without finding anything.

Connie had to go back for tea at six o'clock, but Ruby said she would carry on looking for a while longer as she hadn't finished checking the topmost branches yet. They arranged to meet after dark that night in the library.

When Connie got back to the flat, her aunt and uncle were already tucking into their beans on toast. There were custard tarts for afterwards, which Uncle Maurice had bought that morning in the village. Custard tarts were a favourite of Aunt Alice's, and she was in a very good mood with Uncle Maurice because he

65

had remembered that.

Connie asked after Aunt Alice's boarding-school pupils and Uncle Maurice's dragons and, when they asked what *she* had been doing that afternoon, she replied, as casually as she could, 'Nothing much. I went for a walk to see how big the grounds are.'

'Big, are they?' Uncle Maurice asked, displaying a mouthful of half-chewed beans.

Connie nodded.

'I dread to think what those fitness fanatics are going to do to them,' Aunt Alice sighed. 'Dig them up and build a whole load of tennis courts and swimming pools probably.'

Connie hadn't yet told Ruby that Bluebell Hall was about to be turned into a health club. But if Ruby still hadn't found the ring by the time Connie met her tonight, she was going to have to, and she dreaded to think how Ruby would react.

'I wonder when they'll put the contents of the house up for auction,' Aunt Alice continued. 'I wouldn't mind having a look at some of those books.'

66

'Why don't we just pop in through the window like Connie did and have a browse?' Uncle Maurice suggested.

'We can't do that!' Aunt Alice snapped. 'That would be trespassing.'

'Well, go and ask our dear landlady first then.' He waved a forkful of soggy toast at his niece. 'You were getting on famously with her this morning, weren't you, Connie?'

Connie nodded. 'She was a bit fierce to start with, but she got friendly really quickly when I gave her the flowers.'

Uncle Maurice's face suddenly changed. 'That's it,' he muttered, throwing his fork down on his plate. 'That's perfect! Horatio must be given flowers!' He pushed back his chair and jumped up, bending over to kiss Connie on top of her head. 'You're a genius, Connie.' And he raced off up to his study.

Connie looked in surprise at Aunt Alice. 'Who's Horatio?'

'His dragon—the one who likes jelly babies. He's been trying to think of a way for the boy in his book to make Horatio change from being fierce to

friendly. I expect he's just decided that the way to tame a dragon is to give him flowers.' She laughed and reached out for a custard tart.

'Just like fairies like to be given chocolate,' Connie murmured, before she could stop herself.

Her aunt gave her a fond look. 'We've really got your imagination going while you've been staying with us, haven't we? Maybe there's going to be another author in the family!'

Connie shook her head. 'I don't think so.' Personally, she found it hard enough to sit down long enough to do her homework for school, let alone write a whole book.

When the tea things were cleared away, Aunt Alice suggested a game of Scrabble, which Connie had never played before. By the time they had finished, it was getting late. Connie went upstairs at her usual time and got into bed without getting undressed. Now all she had to do was wait for her aunt and uncle to go to bed too. Aunt Alice never stayed up late and Connie heard her come up not long after she

68

had turned off her own light. But Uncle Maurice remained in his study. Connie knew that her uncle could work late into the night if he was in one of what Aunt Alice called 'his writing frenzies'. Aunt Alice never had writing frenzies herself and she was quite envious of Uncle Maurice's. In the end, Connie got fed up with waiting and decided to leave the house while he was still awake.

Connie crept downstairs and outside, noticing that the fairy bluebells, which had disappeared during the day, were back again.

She hurried round to the library where Ruby was at the window waiting for her. 'I didn't find it.' Ruby sounded anxious. 'It must have had an even happier moment that we don't know about yet. You'll have to go back and speak to the old lady again. There must be some other stories about the ring she can tell you.'

'OK,' Connie quickly agreed. 'But listen, Ruby, there's something else . . .' And she told the fairy how Bluebell Hall was about to be turned

69

into a health club. 'All the books are going to be sold or got rid of. So there's no point in you sorting them out.'

Ruby looked stunned. 'I *have* to sort them out,' she said. 'The fairy queen can't change the punishment spell she put on me. She made it so that the only way I can get back into fairyland is if I return the ring or my task is done. If I can't do the task *or* find the ring, then I'll *never* be able to go home again.'

Connie was shocked. She somehow hadn't imagined that fairy law could be so harsh. 'Well, you've still got a month or two left. If you read non-stop, couldn't you get through all the books in that time?'

Ruby let out a bitter laugh. 'Fairies read fast, but not *that* fast! I've counted all the books in this library. There are two thousand, one hundred and eighty-six. If I read one book a day—and that's fast reading—it will still take me nearly *six years* to read all of them.'

Connie stared at her. 'But what will happen to you if they close the library and you can't go home?'

'I'll be a lost fairy in your world, I

suppose—flying about on my own and never having a home to go to ever again.' Ruby was looking very pale now.

'But that's terrible! We have to find the ring before that happens! I'll go back and see Mrs Fitzpatrick tomorrow. I'll ask her more about the ring's history. Then we'll look in every place where it sounds like the ring might have been happy.'

Ruby bit her lip. She looked like she was about to cry. 'Do you really think we can still find it?'

'I'm positive we can!' Connie replied firmly. She briefly remembered what her uncle had told her about how it was doubtful people who found fairies, not positive ones. But that was fairies, not rings. And, in any case, she doubted that the rule applied to people who were only *pretending* to be positive to cheer up their friend.

6

Connie woke up late the next morning. By the time she got dressed and went downstairs, her aunt and uncle were both writing. Her aunt worked at the table in the living room during the day and Connie saw that she was making slow progress this morning. She could tell this by the number of screwed-up sheets of paper littered around the floor, and by the packet of chocolate digestives on the table beside her that was already almost finished.

Aunt Alice was dropping biscuit

crumbs over her keyboard as she read on the screen the last paragraph she had typed. 'Hopeless!' she hissed, pressing the delete button and getting rid of the whole thing. Then she noticed Connie standing there. 'Oh, hello, darling. I'm not having a very good writing day, I'm afraid.'

'Why don't you come to the village with me?' Connie suggested. 'I want to go and visit Mrs Fitzpatrick.'

'What? Again?'

'Yes.' Connie had already planned what she was going to say to explain herself. 'The nurse said she hardly ever gets any visitors. Anyway, it'll be good for me to walk to the village. Mum says everyone should do at least half an hour of exercise every day to keep themselves fit.'

'Does she?' Aunt Alice, who never took much exercise, looked like that was the last thing she felt like doing. 'Perhaps you'd better go then if—' She broke off, suddenly looking less certain. 'I don't know though. Would your mother let you walk as far as the village on your own?'

Connie hesitated. Her parents hardly let her go anywhere on her own, even though they were sympathetic about the fact that she wanted to. Her mother was always saying it was a shame Connie couldn't have the freedom that she'd had in her own childhood, but that it just wasn't safe to let your children go wandering off alone these days.

Aunt Alice suddenly jumped up. 'Do you know what? I think I will come with you! I'm not getting anywhere with this. What I need is a complete break. But we won't walk, we'll take the car. I want to get some shopping. I can go to the supermarket on the other side of the village.'

'OK,' Connie said. 'Can you drop me off at the old people's home on the

way? Then you can come and pick me up on your way back.'

'Of course—and I might even come in and say hello to Mrs Fitzpatrick myself. I can ask her about the auction then.'

'Oh, and can you buy me some chocolate when you go to the supermarket?' Connie asked. 'Some chocolate buttons or something?'

'I like those new *giant* chocolate buttons myself,' Aunt Alice said. 'Shall I see if they've got some of those?'

'Oh no,' Connie said quickly. 'I want the normal ones, please.' She knew that even an ordinary-sized chocolate button would be gigantic for Ruby.

Her aunt made Connie some breakfast before they set off, then she drove her right up to the front door of Mrs Fitzpatrick's nursing home and waited until a nurse opened it before giving her a wave and leaving her there.

Connie was taken through to the lounge this time where Mrs Fitzpatrick was sitting by the window, holding a magnifying glass to her eye as she peered at the small print in the

75

newspaper. 'They should make large-print newspapers,' she complained grumpily, setting the magnifier down as Connie came over to her. 'Another visit? Didn't I bore you enough the last time?'

Connie shook her head. 'You didn't bore me at all. I really liked it when you told me that story about your ring yesterday. I came to tell you that I found that oak tree. I went there yesterday afternoon.'

'Did you?' The old lady smiled and Connie saw that, despite seeming grumpy, Mrs Fitzpatrick was pleased to see her. 'Did you make a wish?'

'Oh no. I asked Ruby and she said it isn't a real wishing tree. So I didn't bother.'

'Who's Ruby? Knows about these things, does she?' There was an edge of sarcasm in Mrs Fitzpatrick's voice and Connie realized she'd offended her.

'Well, yes,' she murmured, flushing. 'She knows because . . .' Connie stopped herself from finishing. She didn't know how the old lady would react if she told her that Ruby

was a fairy.

'Well, at least you've got a friend to play with,' Mrs Fitzpatrick sighed. 'That's good. Friends are *so* important. Is Ruby your best friend then?'

Connie swallowed. 'Not exactly. My best friend's called Emma, but she lives in Canada.'

'Canada? Well, that's no good, is it? You'd better find a best friend who's nearer than that, hadn't you?'

'No . . . I mean, yes, I suppose, but she's only just moved so . . .' Connie struggled to steer the conversation back to the topic of the ring. 'Anyway, I went with Ruby to see the tree and now I think I'd like to . . . to—' Connie was trying to think up a good reason for being so interested in the ring, when she remembered her aunt and uncle— 'To write a *story* about the ring and everything that's happened to it. So I was thinking if I asked you, you could tell me the whole of its history.'

'I see.' Mrs Fitzpatrick looked amused. 'You know, you remind me of my older sister, Annabel. She was always interested in history. My mother told Annabel everything she knew about that ring so she's the one who was the expert.'

'Can I speak to her then?' Connie asked, eagerly. 'Does she live near here too?' Aunt Alice had told her that Mrs Fitzpatrick didn't have any relatives, but that couldn't be true after all.

'She's dead now, I'm afraid. She died fifteen years ago.' The old lady shook her head sadly, looking at Connie as if trying to decide whether to tell her something else. 'That ring was always handed down to the oldest daughter of the family. My mother intended it to go to Annabel. When our mother died quite suddenly while we were still young—I was only seventeen and Annabel was a couple of years older— my father gave half of my mother's jewellery to me and half to my sister, and it was my half that contained the ring. Annabel pointed out that our mother had wanted her to have it, but my father saw how much I wanted it for myself and claimed he didn't know anything about it. I was always his favourite, you see. So I got to keep the

78

ring and Annabel was very angry with me and refused to tell me any of the stories about it, even though I was interested now that the ring was mine.' Mrs Fitzpatrick stopped talking and looked very far away.

'What happened after that?' Connie prompted her.

'Over the years we became more and more distant. After she got married she went to live in London and I stayed at Bluebell Hall with my father. I was still unmarried and living at home when our father died, and he left the house and all its contents to me. Annabel was very hurt about that and she never spoke to me again afterwards. I invited her and her family—she had a little girl by that time to my own wedding a few years later, but she didn't come. I heard news of her over the years through a cousin who kept in touch with both of us. Apparently Annabel's daughter became a teacher and married another teacher and *they* had a daughter who they named Eliza after my mother. My cousin died a few years back and the last I heard of my sister's

79

family was that her daughter wasn't in very good health and had gone to live at the seaside. Eliza's daughter—that would be my great-niece—was working as a librarian somewhere in London.' She paused. 'I was interested to hear that she was a librarian because we were always a bookish family. You've seen my father's collection of books in the house, haven't you?'

Connie nodded. 'But don't you know any more about the ring than that? Didn't your mother or sister tell you *anything*?'

'I told you. I wasn't interested enough to ask questions before my mother died, and afterwards my sister and I didn't get on. Annabel might have handed down the stories to her own daughter—I don't know. I wish I'd given that ring to Annabel. We might have been closer then.' She sighed. 'I was going to try and make things right by leaving it to her daughter in my will but now that I've lost it, I can't even do that.'

'Maybe someone will find it and bring it back to you,' Connie said.

The old lady shook her head. 'I still think my housekeeper's son took it, though it's done me no good to say that. Ella—that was my housekeeper—was with me for ten years and now I never see her, even though she only lives in the village. Can't blame her, I suppose. Standing up for her boy. But I never trusted him. Stole some money out of his mother's purse once when he was little—she told me so herself.'

Connie frowned. She wanted to say that she knew Ella's son hadn't stolen the ring, but she couldn't say that without giving away how she knew. 'My mum says you should never decide that people are guilty unless you have proper proof.'

'Really? Your mother sounds like my lawyer.'

'She says you shouldn't judge people just by their appearance either,' Connie continued, doggedly.

'Well, she's right there! That boy of Ella's always looked so angelic—blond hair, blue eyes, like butter wouldn't melt in his mouth. Those are the ones you've got to watch out for!'

81

Connie sighed, seeing that she wasn't getting anywhere. 'I'd still really like to find out more about your ring,' she said. 'For my story, I mean. Do you know whereabouts your niece went to live at the seaside? Maybe I could write to her and see if your sister told *her* anything about it.'

'I don't have any contact with Annabel's family any more. All I know about them is what I've already told you. Now, why don't you tell me a bit about *your* family? That fellow who was here yesterday—with those terrible eyebrows—how is he related to you? I must say that you don't look anything like him, thank goodness!'

So Connie told Mrs Fitzpatrick about her mum and dad and Aunt Alice and Uncle Maurice. She told her that her mum was an outdoor, sporty person whereas her aunt was an indoor, bookish person. Connie explained how she used to think she was an outdoor person too, but that she was now beginning to think that libraries were more interesting places than she'd first realized. And, to her surprise, she ended up telling her all about Emma and how much she missed her since she had moved to Canada.

'It sounds as though this Emma was a wonderful friend,' Mrs Fitzpatrick said. 'It seems to me that she's *worth* missing.'

Connie frowned. 'How do you mean?'

'Just that. What you need to do next is to make another friend who you'd miss just as much if *they* went away. Take Hester, who I only met two months ago. I knew she was my friend the day I realized how much I'd miss her if she popped her clogs before I did.' She gave a little laugh.

Connie knew what popping your clogs meant and she didn't think it was anything to joke about. 'It's not that easy making new friends,' she pointed out.

'What about this Ruby you mentioned just now?'

'Oh, she's not a real friend,' Connie said, quickly. She flushed then, realizing how peculiar that sounded.

But Mrs Fitzpatrick looked like she

understood. 'I see . . . an imaginary one, is she? I used to have imaginary friends when I was a girl. They're all very well, but it's true that you do need some real ones too.'

'And it's not easy to make real ones when you're stuck here for the whole school holidays,' Connie added swiftly, eager to avoid further questions about Ruby.

'Well, it won't always be the holidays, will it? There's bound to be a new boy or girl who'll need a new friend too when you go back to school.'

'There *might* be,' Connie agreed. 'But I might not want to be best friends with them. It doesn't mean I'll really get on with someone, just because *they* haven't got a best friend either, does it?'

'Well, in that case, you'll just have to do without a best friend for a bit longer, until you find someone you *do* really get on with, won't you?' Mrs Fitzpatrick replied briskly, and Connie thought she sounded like she was getting a bit bored with the subject of best friends now.

They were drinking tea and munching biscuits and trying to think of other things to talk about when Aunt Alice arrived. Unlike Uncle Maurice, Connie's aunt was very friendly and polite to Mrs Fitzpatrick, who seemed to take to her immediately. When Aunt Alice mentioned her interest in books, the old lady said that she could borrow the key to Bluebell Hall so that she could have a look at the books before they were auctioned. They eventually left, with Aunt Alice leaving a bag of giant chocolate buttons for Mrs Fitzpatrick and whispering, 'Don't worry, Connie. I've got the ones you wanted in the car.'

By the time they got home, Aunt Alice was in what she reckoned was a good mood for writing, so Connie offered to put the shopping away while her aunt got straight back to work. When she'd finished, she put her own chocolate buttons in her pocket and headed for the library where she knew Ruby would be waiting to hear how she had got on.

Ruby was reading a book when she

85

arrived. She stopped as soon as Connie climbed in through the window. 'Well?' she asked eagerly. 'What did you find out?'

Connie thought about giving Ruby the chocolate straight away, then decided to wait and use it to cheer her up after she'd told her the bad news.

'She doesn't know anything else,' Connie began gently. 'Her mother told everything about the ring to her sister, not to her, and her sister's dead. Her sister had a daughter who she might have told things to, but Mrs Fitzpatrick doesn't know where she is.' She stopped and frowned at Ruby. 'So I don't know what else we can do.'

Ruby looked appalled. 'What? She couldn't tell you *anything* else about the ring?'

Connie shook her head. 'Only sad stuff about it. She and her sister fell out over it because her sister was meant to inherit the ring rather than her. And Mrs Fitzpatrick wanted to leave it to her niece in her will—sort of to make things right again but now that she's lost it, she can't. Though I don't really

86

see how she could have got it to her
since she doesn't know where she lives.
All she knows is that her *great*-niece is
a librarian somewhere in London.'

'A librarian?' Ruby was staring at
her.

'That's right.'

'Did she tell you her name?'

'No . . . oh, wait a minute . . . she said
she was named Eliza after Mrs
Fitzpatrick's mother.'

Ruby was looking excited. 'We might
be able to find her. I'll get Sapphire
and Emerald to ask all the fairy
librarians who look after the London
libraries if they've heard of her.'

'*Fairy* librarians?'

'Yes. They're fairies who work in
your libraries. Their main job is to
keep the human librarians from
moving the entry-books and to check
that they don't dust all the fairy dust
off them. Librarians who like to dust a
lot can cause us fairies a lot of
problems.' Ruby flew up to the top
shelf and came back with a notepad
and a miniature gold-coloured pen.
She quickly started to scribble a

87

message in tiny handwriting. 'I'll send this to Sapphire and Emerald right now.'

'How will you send it?' Connie asked, as she watched Ruby fold up the piece of paper and write the names of her two friends on the front.

'I'll post it!' Ruby flew up to a book on one of the middle shelves.

Connie saw that the book was the one she had seen before sparkling. She had tried really hard to spot it every time she visited the library, but, until now she hadn't succeeded. Ruby had told her it was because entry-books tended to camouflage themselves by not sparkling very much when they weren't being used by the fairies. The book was sparkling now as Ruby flew into the gap between it and the shelf above and slipped her letter down between the pages. 'There!' she said.

88

'They should get that straight away.'

'But even if they *do* find out where Mrs Fitzpatrick's great-niece works, how will that help us?' Connie asked, having to struggle to tear her eyes away from the book to look at Ruby, who had now flown into the middle of the room.

'If she's been told stories about the ring, then she can tell us where to look for it, can't she?'

'Are Sapphire and Emerald going to ask her then?'

'Oh no. Even if she's in the right mind for seeing fairies—and only a few grown-up humans ever are—she won't *react* very well to seeing them. Adult humans who see us always think they're going mad and rush straight off to see their doctor before we've even had a chance to open our mouths. It's most irritating. That's why—' Ruby stopped and gave Connie a steady look.

'What?' Connie asked.

'That's why we need *you* to go and talk to her.'

'Me? Don't be silly! How would I get to London? It's too far away!'

89

'Not if you go there through the books.'

'*What?*'

'We *can* take humans through the entry-books with us—just like we can take objects—so long as they want to go. It just isn't something that fairies do very often. It needs a lot of fairy magic and I'd have to ask the fairy queen's permission first.'

Ruby broke off as she noticed the bulge in the pocket of Connie's dress. She flew closer to look, sniffing the air as she went. Fairies had a very good sense of smell, especially when it came to sniffing out chocolate.

'Here,' Connie said, quickly pulling out the chocolate buttons and holding them out to her. 'Ruby, what are you talking about? How could you take me with you? I don't understand.'

'*I* couldn't take you. I'm not allowed to leave here, remember? But you could go through with Sapphire and Emerald.' Ruby had already snatched away the bag of buttons and was flying up towards the top shelf with it balanced on her head like a giant sack.

90

'I'll let you know when they send a reply to my letter. You'd better go now. I have to write another letter—a very important one to the fairy queen—so I need to be left alone to concentrate.'

And she disappeared behind the top row of books and didn't come out again.

7

Connie waited for the rest of the day for Ruby to send her a sign that she had heard back from her two fairy friends. Just before tea she went to the library window and looked in. The window was closed and there were no fairy lights on inside. Connie knocked and called out Ruby's name, but there was no response. Connie returned to the flat, feeling frustrated.

Connie's postcard from Emma, sent on by her mother, had arrived that morning. Connie read it now for the

tenth time and remembered what Mrs Fitzpatrick had said about how it was a good thing to miss someone because it showed they really meant a lot to you. That was all very well, Connie thought, but what if they meant so much that you couldn't imagine anybody else ever taking their place?

Her mother had included a little note of her own:

Dad and I are missing you, darling, but it sounds as though you're having a nice time with Aunt Alice and Uncle Maurice.

Connie had told her mum on the phone that she was enjoying her holiday at Bluebell Hall, although in the end she hadn't mentioned anything about Ruby because she knew her mum wouldn't believe her.

Connie wondered if Mrs Fitzpatrick's great-niece—Eliza—believed in fairies. She hoped so. It would make it much easier to explain things to her if she did.

After tea, when she had finished

helping Aunt Alice with the washing-up, Connie went down to the lake to feed the swans with some old bread that her aunt had been going to throw out. One of the swans swam up to the bread, prodded it a bit with its beak; then swam away again without touching it. The others, one of whom still had its red flower crown sitting lopsidedly on its head, didn't even bother coming to look.

'They like *fresh* bread,' a voice said from behind her. 'How would you like to be given mouldy old bread for *your* tea?'

Connie looked round and saw Ruby. 'It's not mouldy. Anyway, the swans in the park at home eat it.'

'Well, these ones won't. Mrs Fitzpatrick used to feed them fresh French bread every day. Sometimes she made them salmon and cucumber sandwiches.'

Connie smiled. 'I suppose she cut off the crusts as well, did she?'

'Don't be silly—swans *like* crusts! Now listen, I've come to tell you that Sapphire and Emerald have found Mrs

94

Fitzpatrick's great-niece. They've been to have a look at her in her library and they say she looks quite friendly. But *she* couldn't see *them* even though they flew right in front of her nose. So we need you to go and talk to her. You will, won't you?'

'Well, yes, if it'll help, but-—'

'Good! I've already sent a message to the fairy queen and she's going to come to the library to interview you at midnight tonight. You'll have to wear your best dress. And you'd better tidy your hair. And you can't wear those.' She pointed at Connie's trainers. 'Haven't you got some nice *sparkly* shoes to wear?'

Connie frowned. Ruby could get a bit too bossy sometimes. 'I haven't got any sparkly shoes, but I can wear my other trainers—the ones with the flashing lights on the heels. I didn't realize I was going to have an *interview.*'

'Queen Amethyst always has to interview any humans who want to go into fairyland,' Ruby said. 'She's a very important person. You'll have to curtsy

when you meet her. Do you know how to curtsy?'

'Of course I do,' Connie replied. She had seen people curtsying to the real Queen on television, usually when they were presenting her with a bouquet of flowers. Thinking of that gave her an idea. 'Don't worry,' she told Ruby. 'I'll make sure Queen Amethyst likes me. I'll be very respectful.'

Ruby still looked nervous. 'She's quite a scary fairy, you know. Especially when she's telling you off about something. Oh dear. I'd better go and dust the library again before she gets here.' And she zoomed off.

'See you later,' Connie called after her, smiling. She guessed that Ruby had probably got told off quite a lot by Queen Amethyst when she'd lived in fairyland. But she still didn't see why *she* should feel afraid of her. After all, the fairy queen couldn't be all that different from any other fairy, could she?

*   *   *

At midnight, Connie was sitting in the library as Ruby fluttered around still checking anxiously for dust. The fairy lights were on and Connie was sitting cross-legged on the rug staring at the entry-book, which had been sparkling for the last few minutes.

'It's warming up to transport Queen Amethyst,' Ruby explained. 'Sapphire and Emerald are coming as well.'

Connie was holding a bunch of bluebells in her hand, which she had stopped to pick on her way to the library. She had tied some silver ribbon round the stems to make a little bouquet to present to the fairy queen. She had also been practising how to curtsy.

Suddenly Connie saw the entry-book slide off its shelf and open by itself so that it was hovering in the air in front of the bookcase. The page where it had opened began to glow gold and then a beam of light suddenly shot out from the book—as wide as the page itself and as strong as the beam from a very powerful torch.

Then something sparkling and

purple was travelling down the beam towards them, getting clearer and clearer and sharper and sharper as it got closer, like a fuzzy picture gradually coming into focus. As Connie scrambled to her feet, a very grand-looking fairy came flying out from the light. She had long snow-white hair and she was wearing a long purple dress made out of several different layers of crêpe and tissue paper, the outer layer of which was decorated with gold full stops. The dress had long sleeves with frilly tissue-paper cuffs and her waistband was made from a velvet bookmark. Her delicate purple shoes were decorated with sparkly gold exclamation marks (because that was Queen Amethyst's favourite type of punctuation) and on her head she wore a crown made from solid-gold letters of the alphabet all joined together.

'I am Queen Amethyst, queen of the book fairies,' the fairy announced, in a haughty voice. 'You must be Connie.'

Connie stared at her in awe and immediately knew what Ruby meant about her being scary. Her face seemed

older than Ruby's and she had sharp
cheekbones and a pointed chin. Her
eyes were a violet colour and, as she
inspected Connie from head to toe, her
lips remained pressed together sternly.
Connie tried to curtsy, but she was so
nervous that she stumbled and nearly
dropped her flowers.

Queen Amethyst was looking at the
flowers in surprise and Connie

immediately saw her mistake—the bluebells were as huge as trees compared with the fairy queen. She should have brought some tiny flowers instead, like buttercups or violets.

'O-oh . . .' Connie stammered. 'I forgot they'd be . . . that you'd be . . .' But as she spoke, Queen Amethyst rubbed her fingertips together and suddenly the bunch of bluebells was showered with golden dust.

'How splendid,' the fairy queen said, holding out her hand to take the bouquet that, to Connie's amazement, had now magically shrunk in size. Queen Amethyst sniffed the flowers politely, then handed them to one of her fairy assistants (just like the real Queen was always doing when she got given flowers on the television).

Connie had been so busy staring at Queen Amethyst that she hadn't noticed the other two fairies who had emerged from the beam of light behind her. There was one with a blue dress and shiny dark hair, who Connie took to be Sapphire, and one with wavy blonde hair and a green dress, who she

guessed must be Emerald, the fairy who was jumpy around humans. Queen Amethyst handed her bouquet to Sapphire, then started to fly around the library inspecting all the books and running her finger along some of them to check for dust. Connie saw that Ruby had been right to do all that extra dusting earlier on.

Finally, the fairy queen landed on the window ledge and told them all to sit. She stretched out her wings and stood there looking down at them. 'Now,' she began, 'Ruby has told me about her plan to return the ring to its rightful owner. I understand that Connie wishes to help and that to do so she must travel through the entry-book. Is that correct?'

Ruby nodded. 'Yes, your majesty.'

The queen looked at Connie. And you are sure that you want to do this?'

Connie gulped. 'Yes—if it's possible.'

'It is certainly *possible*, but it is up to me to decide if it is *advisable.*' She peered at Connie sharply. 'First, I must decide if I can trust you.'

'I promise I'll never tell anyone about the entry-book,' Connie said quickly. 'I'll keep it a secret always.'

Queen Amethyst looked solemn. 'I have interviewed children before who wanted to enter fairyland. I have not permitted it if I did not like their answers to my questions. It will be the same for you.' She paused. 'I have three questions to ask that will help me decide in your case and they must be answered *truthfully.*'

Connie immediately felt even more nervous. She hadn't realized that she was going to have to pass some sort of test in order to be allowed to help Ruby.

'Question number one,' Queen Amethyst began briskly. 'Which do you prefer—watching television or reading books?'

Connie felt slightly sick. She knew which answer the queen of the book fairies would like best, but how could she say it when it wasn't true? OK, so she had got a bit more interested in reading since she came to stay with her aunt and uncle, but only because they didn't have a television set. She still liked to watch television much more. 'Television,' mumbled Connie, going bright red.

'I beg your pardon? Speak up!' Queen Amethyst looked very fierce, as if she had heard Connie's answer but didn't want to believe it.

'Television,' Connie repeated, so loudly that she made Ruby jump.

There was a long pause and Connie didn't dare to look at Ruby, who had

103

let out a little gasp of dismay as she spoke. Then the queen asked her second question. 'You have promised never to tell anyone about the entry-book. But do you *always* keep your promises, Connie?'

Connie nearly replied 'yes', straight away. Then she remembered a promise she had made to Emma once. She had promised not to tell anybody that Emma was being bullied by this other girl at school. Emma hadn't wanted her to tell but in the end Connie had broken her promise to Emma and told their teacher. Emma had been angry when she'd found out but, when the bullying had stopped, Emma had forgiven her.

'Well . . .' Connie began. 'I *usually* keep my promises but sometimes—'

'Yes or no?' Queen Amethyst snapped impatiently. 'Do you *always* keep your promises, or do you not?'

Connie gulped. 'No,' she said, 'not *always*, but—'

The fairy queen held up her hand for silence. 'My final question is this—who would you rather have as your best

104

friend? A fairy or a human?'

Connie thought about that carefully. Ruby had become her best friend since Emma had left but, if she were given the choice to have Emma back again, what would she say? She thought about all the fun she'd been having with Ruby recently. Then she thought about her life back at home when Emma had been there. She'd gone to school with Emma, seen her nearly every weekend, and had lots of sleepovers at Emma's house or hers when the two of them had stayed awake whispering to each other about all sorts of things late into the night. The thing was, she missed Emma really badly. Emma was like the sister she'd never had. She couldn't imagine ever making another friend like her.

'I'd want Emma,' Connie whispered.

'Then you would rather have a human,' Queen Amethyst said crisply.

Connie bit her lip, glancing at Ruby. She felt terrible. The last thing she wanted to do was hurt her fairy friend's feelings. The queen had ordered her to tell the truth and she had done that,

but now she was starting to wish that she had lied. Surely it was better to lie sometimes, if it meant that you didn't hurt anybody and you could get what you wanted—especially if the thing that you wanted was going to help somebody else and not just yourself? As it was, she was certain that her answers weren't the ones that the fairy queen wanted to hear and, since Queen Amethyst had refused entry to other children because she hadn't liked their answers, she was quite likely to do the same to her. Then what would happen to Ruby?

'Well, Connie . . .' Queen Amethyst sighed, flying off the window ledge and hovering in the air. 'It is a shame that you are a strange child who prefers television to books and human friends to fairy friends.'

'Does that mean she hasn't passed the test?' Ruby asked, sounding upset.

Connie, who was staring at her toes because she was too embarrassed to face the fairy queen's piercing gaze, looked up.

Queen Amethyst was frowning. 'I

106

shall have to think very carefully about this. It can be dangerous to perform the shrinking spell on a human who is unsuitable. I will let you know at nine o'clock tomorrow morning.'

'Shrinking spell?' Connie queried, but the fairy queen was already beckoning to Emerald and Sapphire to accompany her back into the beam of light so that they could go home.

Connie watched, mesmerized, as the three fairies disappeared back along the light beam and into the book. Then the entry-book slammed itself shut and floated back to its place on the shelf. Connie stared at it, completely speechless.

She remembered an expression her mother sometimes used if she caught Connie daydreaming: *Is that you away wi' the fairies again?* It was a saying Connie's mother had learnt from her Irish grandmother.

Well, tomorrow, if the fairy queen decided that she had passed the test, she definitely *would* be away with the fairies. Only this time it would be for real. She would be going away with them inside that magic book. But how could she have passed the test with the answers she had given?

'Oh, Ruby, I'm so sorry,' Connie burst out, as soon as they were alone together.

Ruby was looking very cross. 'I told you, you should've worn sparkly shoes!' she snapped. 'You have no interview skills at all!'

'Shall I come back here at nine o'clock tomorrow then?'

'If you like. Though I don't see that it'll do much good now!'

And, after that, she flew back up to her top shelf and wouldn't speak to Connie again.

8

Connie was dreaming that she had been shrunk down to the size of a mouse and that Uncle Maurice was about to tread on her. She could hear his heavy footsteps thudding towards her and, however loudly she shouted to tell him she was there, her voice would only come out as a whisper.

'Connie!' Her bedroom door was pushed open and Connie woke up with a start, realizing that the thudding sound had been her uncle knocking on her door. 'Aunt Alice wants to know if you'd like to come with us to see Mrs Fitzpatrick's library.'

'What? Now?' Connie looked at her bedside clock. It was already ten-past eight. At nine o'clock she was meeting Ruby and Queen Amethyst in the library. Her stomach felt queasy as she remembered the reason she was meeting them. If only her interview with the fairy queen had gone better.

'Yes. I'm in between chapters and you know that's the only time I can concentrate on anything else. Hurry up and get dressed and you can come with us.'

'It's OK. I want some breakfast first,' Connie said quickly. 'I might come over later.' Maybe if her aunt and uncle went right now, they would have left the library by the time Queen Amethyst arrived.

As soon as she was left alone, Connie got washed and dressed and made herself some toast, although she was far too nervous to eat it. Then, when her aunt and uncle didn't return after half an hour, she headed for the library herself. This time she entered

Bluebell Hall through the front door, which had been left open for her. Mrs Fitzpatrick was right—the grand old hallway, with its Chinese rugs and stained-glass windows, was a very impressive sight indeed.

Connie spotted Ruby straight away, sliding down the curved wooden banister towards her. Ruby had been polishing it to make it more slippery

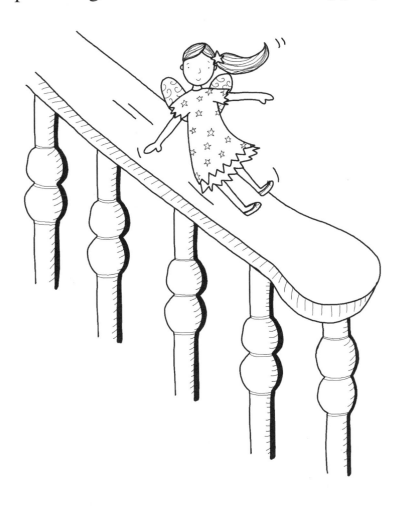

and now she shouted out in delight as she shot off the end. Connie was relieved to see that Ruby seemed to have cheered up since last night, but she was still dreading how her friend would react if the fairy queen said Connie had failed the test. What if Ruby got so cross that she never wanted to see her again? 'Is that you, Connie?' Uncle Maurice called out from the library, even though Connie hadn't made any sound at all yet.

'Do you think he heard *me?*' whispered Ruby, fluttering to a halt in mid-air. 'If he can hear me, he might be able to see me. I'd better keep out of his way. We don't want to give him a fright.'

Somehow Connie didn't think Uncle Maurice was the type of person to get a fright if he met a fairy—or even a dragon for that matter—but she didn't say that to Ruby. She didn't want to complicate things by letting Uncle Maurice in on their secret. Knowing him, he'd probably want to get shrunk down in size himself and come to fairyland with them.

112

Connie walked into the library, anxious to see how her aunt and uncle were getting on. Surely they couldn't be going to spend much longer here. After all, unless you knew about the fairies, this was just a musty room full of boring old books. But, of course, she should have known that Aunt Alice and Uncle Maurice wouldn't see it like that. Her aunt was in raptures over some huge old book of poems she had found and her uncle was balancing precariously on an antique wooden chair trying to reach the books on the top shelf. He was alarmingly near where Ruby kept all her things.

'This is wonderful. I could stay here all day,' Aunt Alice enthused.

Uncle Maurice grunted and pulled out a half-empty packet of chocolate buttons from behind one of the books. 'How did these get here?'

Connie tried to distract him by pointing to a big red encyclopedia on the opposite wall. 'Can you get that down for me, Uncle Maurice? I'd really like to have a look at it.'

Her uncle stayed put, spotting

113

another title that interested him, and Aunt Alice, who was just tall enough to reach the encyclopedia, went over to fetch it for her instead. 'I expect its got some interesting pictures in it, Connie. Oh, look,' she gushed, pointing to a black and white drawing of a weird-looking contraption with a huge back wheel. 'Here's a penny-farthing bicycle.'

Connie pretended to be interested, but really she was looking round the shelves for the entry-book. At the moment she couldn't see it. She was sure that Uncle Maurice—who was the only grown-up she knew who believed in fairies—would be able to see it if it started sparkling. Then he would get over-excited and ask lots of questions. What if he insisted on staying to meet the fairy queen himself? And what if Queen Amethyst didn't like him? Lots of people didn't like Uncle Maurice when they first met him because he tended to be quite rude and only want to have conversations about dragons or whatever other weird creature he was writing about at the time.

Connie slipped out into the hallway and found Ruby. 'We've got to get rid of them,' she whispered, looking at the grandfather clock in the corner that showed that it was fast approaching nine o'clock. 'Can't you do something by magic to make them leave?'

Ruby thought about it. 'I could give them measles. Would that help?'

'I don't want you to make them *ill*,' Connie protested. 'Can't you give them something *nice* to make them go away?' She suddenly thought about Uncle Maurice being in between chapters and about Aunt Alice always getting writer's block. 'I know! Why don't you give them some really good *ideas*!'

Ruby looked like she didn't understand.

'For their stories! Then they'll have to rush off to write them down before they forget them, won't they?'

'Hmm . . . I suppose it might work.' Ruby asked Connie what her aunt and uncle's stories were about, then she flew into the library, taking care to sneak up behind Uncle Maurice to

115

avoid being seen. She sprinkled a handful of fairy dust over his head, then went and did the same to Aunt Alice.

Connie watched from the doorway. It wasn't long before her uncle stopped studying the book he was reading and began to look around the room as if he were searching for something. 'You haven't got any paper on you, have you, Alice?'

Aunt Alice had closed the encyclopedia now. 'Funnily enough, I was just thinking that myself. I need to jot something down.' She sounded excited. 'I've been stuck at the same part of my book for ages now, and I've just thought how I can turn it around. If I make the children find a stolen

116

painting of Saint George and the dragon behind the school blackboard, then—'

'I've just thought of a brilliant way of starting my next chapter,' Uncle Maurice interrupted her as he searched in his pockets for a pen. 'That dragon of mine will be sent to boarding school. A boarding school for dragons! Its perfect!'

'I think you must have got their spells mixed up,' Connie whispered to Ruby. 'But it doesn't matter. It's working anyway.'

Her aunt and uncle were already putting back the books they had taken out and getting ready to leave.

'I'd like to stay here for a bit longer,' Connie told them. 'I'll be very careful.'

Ruby's fairy dust must have done more to their thinking than Connie had realized because, instead of the argument she'd expected about how she was too young to be left on her own with all these valuable books, Aunt Alice just tossed her the front door key and told her to be sure to lock up properly. Her aunt and uncle looked bursting with ideas as they raced back to the flat.

'Phew!' said Connie. 'Just in time!'

Not very long after that, the entry-book began to sparkle again and they knew that Queen Amethyst was about to arrive.

*   *   *

'My decision has been difficult,' the fairy queen announced solemnly. 'I was disappointed with your answers to my questions at first, Connie, but on reflection I think the most important thing is that you had the courage to answer them truthfully. Because of that, I know I can trust you. My decision, therefore, is that you have passed the test.'

Ruby let out a triumphant cry and Connie found that she couldn't swallow. There was a huge lump in her throat and she was far too full of emotion to be able to speak. She was being allowed into fairyland after all!

Ruby was flying in circles around the room now, laughing gleefully, and

118

Sapphire and Emerald, who were hovering on either side of the fairy queen, were both grinning too.

Queen Amethyst clapped her hands to restore order. 'We have no time to lose! We must perform the m a g i c s h r i n k i n g s t r a i g h t away!'

Connie felt herself starting to tremble as the fairy queen pointed a long thin finger at her and ordered her to stand still. She then instructed the three younger fairies to hold open a book for Connie to read. It was a book about a little girl who loved reading and wore sparkly shoes. Connie could tell that Queen Amethyst thought all little girls should be like

119

that one.

'Concentrate only on the words in the book,' Queen Amethyst ordered, as she started to fly around Connie's head sprinkling her with fairy dust. 'Keep reading. Read out loud if you want to. But you musn't stop until I tell you.'

As Connie read, she noticed something very strange. The words in the book seemed to be getting bigger and bigger.

Then she realized that the whole book was getting bigger and so were the three fairies who were holding it. Soon she was having to move further back from the page in order to keep the words in focus.

'Close your eyes now,' Queen Amethyst told her, 'but keep walking backwards.'

'I'll bump into the wall,' Connie protested.

'No, you won't. It will take you a long time to reach the edge of the room now. Just do as I say. You must take twenty-six steps back—one for each letter of the alphabet. The fairy dust will turn them into magic steps.'

Connie kept her eyes tightly shut as she moved backwards, one step at a time. It was hard not to open them just a little bit to peek out, but she knew that she mustn't.

'Well done! You can open your eyes now,' the fairy queen said, after she had counted to twenty-six.

Connie opened them and it was as if she were in an entirely different place. The room in which she was standing seemed to extend for miles around her. The other fairies were waving at her from the other side of a huge stretch of rug, still holding the book, which was twice their height.

'You're the same size as us now,' Ruby said, flying over to her. 'You haven't got any wings, but don't worry. You can hold our hands and fly with us that way.'

She took Connie's hand, gave it a little tug to pull her off the ground, and began to tow Connie through the air after her, back to where the other fairies were waiting.

'Listen carefully,' said Queen Amethyst, who was taller than Connie

121

now and even more majestic-looking. 'Sapphire and Emerald will take you through the entry-book into fairyland. From there, it is possible to visit any library in the world. They will show you which one you need to go to.'

'Any library in the world?' gasped Connie, whose head was still swimming with the shock of being reduced to fairy size.

'So long as its entry-book hasn't been lent out to anyone,' Ruby put in. 'They're meant to be kept in the reference section so that people can't take them out of the library, but sometimes—'

'You must go *now*, Connie,' the fairy queen interrupted impatiently. 'The magic shrinking spell will only last for a few minutes if a person is outside fairyland. If you stay here much longer it will wear off. Once you reach the other library, you will return to your normal size.'

'OK,' Connie said. 'But what about when I want to come back again?'

'Emerald and Sapphire will see to that. A human who has been shrunk

122

once is not as difficult to shrink a second time. They should be able to do it without my help. Now off you go.'

Sapphire flew up straight away to take Connie's hand, but Emerald held back.

'It's all right,' Connie told the blonde fairy, giving her what she hoped was a reassuring smile. 'I promise I'm not the sort of human who throws tomato soup at fairies.'

Emerald gave her a nervous smile in return and flew over to her. The entry-book had opened again and, as they travelled together into the light beam, the brightness was so blinding that Connie couldn't see anything.

*   *   *

Connie tried to speak but, just like in her dream that morning, her voice wouldn't come. Then, as her eyes adjusted, she saw that they were flying towards a solid wall of gold. There was a huge letter O written on the wall and it seemed to be increasing in size as they flew towards it. Just as they were

123

almost there, the middle popped out of the O and they were shooting straight through it and out the other side.

'We're here!' Sapphire gasped, laughing as they glided to a halt. 'What do you think?'

Connie stared around her in amazement, totally speechless. They had arrived here in less than a minute. She felt dizzy. And whatever she had been expecting, it hadn't been this.

They seemed to be in a fairy back garden, standing on a rectangle of bright-green grass. The lawn was bordered by flower beds full of bluebells, just like the ones Ruby had made grow by magic outside Bluebell Hall. A washing line was strung from one end of the garden to the other. On it were pegged what looked like sheets, but which were actually the pages of books hanging out to dry.

'It's part of our job to look after the books in the libraries,' Sapphire explained. 'Sometimes we give them a bath. They're always very grateful because human librarians can't do that.

We use special magic water, you see, which means they don't get ruined when they get wet.'

Connie looked behind her and saw a small house with a bright-purple back door. The colours all seemed brighter here, especially the fairies' clothes. Sapphire's pastel-coloured dress was a much more vivid shade of blue now, and Emerald's was a much bolder green. Connie looked down at what she was wearing. Her jeans were less faded and her pale-yellow jumper now looked as bright as the sun.

125

'Can you imagine how brilliant that ruby ring would have looked if it had come here?' Sapphire said, wistfully. 'No wonder Ruby wanted to bring it.'

'Come on,' said Emerald, sounding much more confident now that she was back in fairyland. 'The library we want is this way.'

She led them out through a door in the garden wall, into a park that looked like the sort of place Connie might have drawn with her crayons when she was little. The grass was bright green and the sky was turquoise blue, with white cotton-wool clouds. The trees all had smooth brown trunks and bushy green foliage on top. Nestled in the foliage were rosy red apples and golden yellow pears, which looked ripe enough to eat.

Fairies were dotted about the park in little groups, reading or sunbathing. As Connie looked at them, she noticed something odd. They had funny-coloured hair. A lot of them had black hair like Sapphire and a few had red hair like Ruby, but there were a lot with blue hair and some even had hair

that was green. Sapphire saw Connie staring and explained. 'Book fairies have hair the same colour as ink. That's why it's mostly black or blue, though a few of us are red-heads or green-heads. You'll never see a blonde book fairy though.'

'*Excuse me,*' Emerald said huffily, pointing to her golden curls.

'Except Emerald, of course,' Sapphire added. 'But she's not a natural blonde. She dyes it. She's got green hair underneath. She looks really silly when her roots start to show!'

'I do not!'

'Yes, you do!'

As they argued, Connie noticed three fairies with blue hair sitting together on the nearby grass having a picnic. They were waving to her and smiling as if they knew her.

'Who are they?' she asked Sapphire and Emerald, as she waved back.

Sapphire turned to look. 'They're Canadian book fairies,' she explained. 'Much friendlier that English ones. They're always waving to complete strangers.'

127

'*Canadian* fairies?' Connie felt excited. 'Can we ask them if they know Emma? She's bound to have gone to a library in Canada.'

'There's no time to stop now, but don't worry. There are always loads of Canadian fairies hanging out in this park because there's a really long street of Canadian entry-books near here. We can go and talk to them on the way back if you like.'

'A *street* of entry-books?' Connie queried, thinking that sounded very odd.

'That's right. Like you get streets of houses. The entry-book *we* need is one of those over there. See those ones that back on to the park?'

Connie saw then, that what at first sight looked like a row of terraced houses on the other side of the park, was in fact a row of giant books, the backs of which contained little doors and windows. The windows all had brightly painted shutters and window boxes underneath full of flowers.

'The doors lead to the libraries,' Sapphire explained. 'But the windows

are just for decoration. Pretty, aren't
they?' And she led the way across the
grass.

9

'This is the fairy librarian who works in
the same library as Eliza,' Sapphire
said, introducing Connie to a fairy in a
yellow dress, who had come to meet
them just outside the door of one of
the book-houses. The fairy had long,
black curly hair and looked very similar
to the other fairies, except that she
wore a badge with the word
LIBRARIAN printed on it in gold
letters. It reminded Connie of the
badges the class librarians wore at
school.

'When we go through the door, the beam will take us to the library,' the fairy explained. 'As you can see, the door is quite narrow so it's best if we go through one by one. I've put a wastepaper basket at the other end to give Connie a soft landing.' She slipped a gold key into the lock, turned it and opened the door.

Connie gasped. A beam of light that started at the door and was as high and as wide as the doorway itself, seemed to stretch inwards into the house, except that there was no house on the other side of the door. There was nothing but the lightbeam.

'I'll go first.' The fairy librarian stepped over the doorstep, became a glowing yellow colour for a few moments, then accelerated away from them along the beam pathway.

'You go next,' Sapphire told Connie.

Connie stepped forward nervously and found herself surrounded by light just like before, only this time it was a bit scarier since she didn't have the hands of the two fairies to hold on to. But before she had time to think, she

131

was being whooshed at top speed along the beam and then, after only a minute or two, the light was gone and she felt herself falling through the air. She landed with a bump in a huge heap of scrunched-up giant balls of paper.

'Are you all right?' a fairy voice called out to her.

Connie, who was struggling to see anything over the top of all the paper, cried out, 'Please can you help me out of here?'

The fairy librarian flew down to grab both of Connie's hands. She pulled her up and out of the giant basket to land safely on the floor, by which time, Emerald and Sapphire had arrived too.

'In a few minutes the shrinking spell should wear off and then you can go and find Eliza,' Sapphire told her.

Connie expected that the shrinking spell would wear off gradually and that she would get bigger very slowly, bit by bit. But that didn't happen. Instead, one second she was leaning against the spine of a huge book with her fairy friends on either side of her, and the next, she was in a completely different place—or so it seemed—leaning against a bookshelf in a huge round room. Her three fairy companions were still with her, but she had to look down at her feet to see them.

She seemed to be on a narrow

balcony that ran round the entire wall of the room. She could see lots of old-fashioned desks below her where people were sitting reading, and a central desk, raised up higher than the others, where a librarian was sitting. Connie looked up at the ceiling and held her breath because, even for somebody who was human-sized, the huge gold and blue domed ceiling of the library was awesome. It had a glass window in the top and more windows lower down.

The balcony on which she was standing was the higher of two that ran round the book-lined walls. She looked for a staircase leading up to it from below, but there wasn't one. And nobody seemed to be on either of the balconies except her.

A grey-haired woman who obviously worked there was rushing towards her, waving her arms about. 'How did you get up there?' she shouted up to her crossly. 'Nobody is allowed up there.'

Everyone in the library seemed to have stopped what they were doing to look up at her.

134

'Sapphire! Emerald!' Connie whispered desperately. 'Help me!'

But instead of helping, the three fairies just giggled and flew off the balcony. 'WOW!' Connie heard Emerald gasp in an excited voice. 'This is the coolest library ever! Let's fly right to the top.'

Connie could see two men in brown uniforms entering the main door as she looked round again for a way to climb down. The security guards quickly joined the librarian and Connie heard them ask how they could get up on to the top balcony. Connie saw the women point to a concealed door in one of the wooden wall panels.

Just then a loud gasp went up. Connie looked up with everybody else and saw that the dome above was totally filled with a bright sparkly dust.

As the cloud of fairy dust floated downwards to reach first the balconies, then the reading room itself, everything it touched seemed to light up. The books, the reading desks, people's clothes, even their faces, all started glowing. And then—in the time it took

135

her to blink—Connie found that she was no longer alone on the top balcony, but sitting at a desk with lots of other people on the ground floor. After a few more blinks, the fairy-dust cloud had vanished and the library had returned to normal apart from the two security guards who were still standing staring upwards, looking confused.

'Yes? Can I help you?' the librarian asked them, as if she had totally forgotten what had just happened.

Connie saw that everyone else in the library had gone back to what they had previously been doing—reading or working on the computers—as if their memories of the last few minutes had been completely wiped out too. Fairy dust was obviously pretty strong stuff. She looked up and could just make out three little specks of green, blue and yellow, whizzing around the dome far above them.

As the librarian walked past her, she remembered why she was here and jumped up from her seat. 'Excuse me,' she began. 'I'm . . . I'm looking for a librarian who works here called Eliza.'

136

For an awful moment Connie thought that this fierce-looking woman was going to turn out to be Mrs Fitzpatrick's great-niece—gone prematurely grey from being so bad-tempered—but, after staring at Connie suspiciously for a second or two, she replied, in a loud whisper, 'Eliza is over at the main desk.' She pointed towards a much younger woman with dark hair who was sitting at the desk in the centre of the room.

Connie hurried over, starting to run through in her mind what she was going to say when she got there. It was all very well for Ruby to send her off to speak to Eliza and find out about the ring, but it might have helped if she'd suggested a few ways for her to bring up the subject. As it was, Connie had ended up having to plan what she was going to say herself, and she wasn't sure how convincing it was going to sound.

Connie went and stood in front of the desk. The young woman looked up at her and smiled. 'Yes?'

'Eliza?' Connie asked nervously.

137

'That's right. Can I help you?'

'You don't know me,' Connie continued quickly, 'but I know your great-aunt, Mrs Fitzpatrick. She wanted me to come and say hello.'

'My great-aunt?' Eliza was frowning as if she couldn't think who Connie meant.

'Yes. She's your mother's aunt. She lives in a big house called Bluebell Hall—at least, she used to.'

That seemed to jog the librarian's memory. 'Oh, I know. My grandmother told me about that place, but I've never been there or met my great-aunt. How did she find out that I worked here?'

'Because . . .' Connie faltered, but only for a second. 'Because her cousin told her. I'm staying at Bluebell Hall with my aunt and uncle. I met Mrs Fitzpatrick and she told me about her family and about her ruby ring. It was a sort of family treasure that was handed down from generation to generation. I'm doing a project about history and antique stuff, you see, and she thought you or your mother might be able to tell me more about the ring.'

138

Eliza was looking even more surprised now. 'Are you talking about the famous ring that caused the big family feud? The one that made Grandma and her sister stop speaking to each other?'

'Yes. Mrs Fitzpatrick feels really bad about that now. The thing is, she's lost the ring so I said . . . I said I'd write a story about it for her instead. And she told me that the person who knew most about it was her sister, only she was dead, but that she might have told *her* daughter about it—your mother. And we didn't know where she lived but we knew where to find you. So . . . since . . . since I was coming to London to visit . . . I-I thought I'd ask you if you could ask your mother.'

'My mother's dead now too, I'm afraid,' Eliza said. 'She died last year.'

'Oh.' Connie flushed bright red, but Eliza continued swiftly.

'My grandmother used to tell *me* stories about the special family ring though. I probably know more about it than my mother did. Mum was never as interested as I was in family history.'

'Can *you* tell me about it then?' Connie asked, starting to feel excited again.

'Well, yes . . . I guess I can. But wait a minute—this is all really weird. Who's here with you?'

Connie paused, feeling her heart starting to thump. 'Er . . . Sapphire,' she replied

Eliza started to look around as if she expected a responsible adult to appear from behind the books and introduce herself 'Is she your childminder?'

Connie nodded. (Well, it wasn't a total lie. Sapphire and Emerald *were* her minders—in a way.) 'She . . . er . thought I should come and speak to you myself.'

Well, listen . . . I get a break at eleven o'clock. Can you get Sapphire to bring you back then? I could meet you in the cafe in the courtyard—the one on that side.' She pointed to her left. 'I expect you'll want to have a look round the museum while you're waiting, won't you? The Egyptian stuff is really good.'

'What museum?' Connie asked.

'This one, of course. This is the

140

reading room in the British Museum!'

Oh.' Connie glanced up again to look at the magnificent domed ceiling. She couldn't see any sign of the fairies up there now She quickly agreed to meet Eliza in the cafe and slipped away, saying that Sapphire would be waiting for her. She felt bad about telling so many lies, but she couldn't see how else she could get Eliza to tell her what they needed to know.

Outside the library she found herself with lots of tourists in a very bright indoor courtyard. The courtyard had white walls and a white marble floor and its roof was made up of triangular panes of glass, all fitting together to make a huge glass ceiling. The white library building had two wide white staircases curving up in each direction round its outside, leading to a restaurant at the top.

Connie followed some signs pointing towards the Egyptian section of the museum. As it was the summer holidays, there were lots of people here with children, so Connie didn't look out of place as she crossed the courtyard.

Connie took her time looking round the colossal statues of sphinxes and falcons and ancient Egyptians, then found her way to the rooms where they kept the Egyptian mummies and stone coffins. She was so busy studying a diagram that showed how to embalm a body and prepare it for the afterlife that she hardly noticed the time passing. She was surprised when she looked at her watch and found that it was nearly eleven o'clock.

She easily found the right cafe and Eliza appeared a few minutes after eleven, carrying a paper cup of coffee. She sat down on the bench beside Connie and asked, 'Where's your childminder then?'

'Sapphire's in the library,' Connie said. 'She really likes that domed ceiling. Don't worry. She knows that I'm meeting you here.'

'Hmm.' Eliza took a sip of her drink. 'Well, I'm still feeling really shocked by all of this. I mean, it's incredible—you knowing my great-aunt and coming here and looking me up. I didn't even

know my mother's aunt was still alive, let alone aware of *my* existence.

'Her cousin told her about you before she died,' Connie said. 'Mrs Fitzpatrick doesn't have any other relatives. She doesn't get many visitors. I think she upsets people quite a lot, but I don't think she means to. I think she's quite lonely really.'

'Oh dear,' Eliza sighed. 'Now you're making me feel guilty for not visiting her myself. But my mother always said that if we ever tried to get in touch, she was bound to think we were just after her mon—' Eliza stopped abruptly, obviously having second thoughts about confiding this to Connie who she had, after all, only just met.

'Don't worry,' Connie said quickly. 'Mrs Fitzpatrick couldn't possibly think that now, because she hasn't got any money any more. All she's got is Bluebell Hall and she's selling that to pay for her nursing home.'

'She's in a nursing home?'

'Yes. She fell down the stairs and broke her hip so now she's in a wheelchair.'

'Oh dear.' Eliza was silent for a few moments. Then she said, 'You must like her a lot to be doing all this for her.'

'I like—' Connie stopped herself just in time. She had been about to say that she liked *Ruby* a lot and that was the reason why she was doing this. But it was true that she quite liked Mrs Fitzpatrick too. 'I do like her. So can you tell me some stories about the ring then?'

Eliza nodded. 'My grandmother talked about that ring all the time. She could go on for hours about it. Let's see now . . . There was the story about the wishing tree and how it grew from the spot where the ring was first given to one of Grandma's ancestors. That was a good one. And there was the story about how the ring was used in a secret engagement in the bluebell woods. Or there's my favourite story, about how Grandma's grandmother— my great-*great*-grandmother—went for a midnight swim in the lake and lost the ring until the fairies found it for her.'

'The *fairies* found it?'

'That's right—they left it for her in the fairy fountain.'

'Wait,' Connie said, getting out the notebook she'd brought with her. 'What fairy fountain?'

'The one in the middle of the lake. When it was found, the ring was gleaming so brightly that everyone said the fairies must have rescued it from the lake and polished it before leaving it there for my great-great-grandmother to find. Everyone in her family believed in fairies except her, so the story goes, but on that day, after her ring appeared again, she started to believe in them too. And after that, the family always called that fountain, the fairy fountain.'

Connie was flushed with excitement as she jotted down what Eliza had said. Because surely *this* was the information she had been looking for? Surely *this* must have been the ring's happiest moment?

But even so, she made sure Eliza told her every other story she knew about the ring, just in case.

10

Sapphire and Emerald took Connie back into fairyland where Queen Amethyst met them, looking worried. She said that Connie must return to Ruby's library without delay and that there was no time for her to stop and speak to any of the Canadian fairies about Emma. She had just declared the Bluebell Hall library out of bounds to all other fairies.

'Ruby will explain why when you get there,' the fairy queen told her.

Once she got back, Connie waited a

few minutes for the shrinking spell to wear off, and when she was her normal size again—feeling a little dizzy from all the shrinking and unshrinking—the first thing she noticed was that the books on one side of the library were missing.

'Ruby, where are you?' she called out. 'And what's happened to the books?' As Ruby flew into view, she added, 'I think the ring is in the fountain! Come on! I'll tell you everything on the way there—and you'd better tell me what's been happening here!'

'Connie, I've been so frightened,' Ruby gushed, as soon as they got outside. 'Mrs Fitzpatrick's lawyer came with another man just after you'd gone this morning and they started packing the books up. They're coming back again on Monday to do the rest. I thought they were going to take the entry-book away today. So did Queen Amethyst. That's why she won't let any of the other fairies come here any more. She says it's too dangerous because they could get stuck here.'

147

'That's terrible!' Connie calculated that, as it was now Friday, they had three more days to get Ruby safely back to fairyland. 'But listen to what I found out.' She told Ruby what Eliza had told her about the ring. 'So if I'm right and we find the ring in the fountain and take it back to Mrs Fitzpatrick, you'll be able to go home straight away, won't you?'

Ruby was beaming now. 'Oh, Connie, that's wonderful! I can't wait!'

Despite being pleased for Ruby, Connie couldn't help feeling a little bit sad. She had been hoping that Ruby would say she would miss Connie when she went back to fairyland. Connie would certainly miss *her*, but maybe fairies didn't miss people the way humans did.

When Connie and Ruby got to the lake they found Uncle Maurice standing there with his back to them. Ruby quickly hid behind a bush.

Uncle Maurice whirled round and narrowed his eyes when he saw Connie. 'Where have you been?' he demanded. 'Your aunt is really worried about you!

She's gone to look for you in the village and she's sent me to search the grounds.'

'I was still in the big house,' Connie mumbled.

'We looked for you in the house. Didn't you hear us calling you?'

Connie shook her head, flushing. 'I ... sort of got stuck in a book.'

'Really?'

Uncle Maurice looked as if he thought that was most unlikely.

'Sorry.'

'I haven't had any peace since your aunt got it into her head that you were missing! I told her you'd show up, but she still wouldn't calm down—too vivid an imagination, that's her problem! We'd better go and find her straight away and let her know you're safe.'

'Do we have to go right now?' Connie asked, looking out at the fountain in the middle of the lake. Various jets of water were spurting out of the stone statue of two cherubs clutching a fish, but Connie couldn't see anything red and sparkly that might be a ruby ring.

'Of course we do!' Connie's uncle looked quite cross and Connie knew that she had no choice but to go with him.

As they headed away from the lake, Connie turned back to see Ruby flying out over the water towards the fountain. Hopefully, Ruby would find the ring by herself.

Then she had a horrible thought. What if Ruby found the ring straight away, returned it to Mrs Fitzpatrick and went back to fairyland without waiting to say goodbye to her?

The walk along the road to the village seemed to last for ever, and all the time Connie was thinking about Ruby and what she would do when she found the ring. Then, when they were halfway there, they met Aunt Alice in the car on her way back to Bluebell Hall. She screeched the car to a halt and threw open her door. 'Where on earth have you been, Connie? I've been worried sick! I thought you might have gone to see Mrs Fitzpatrick again so I went there and she kept me talking for so long, I thought I'd never get away.'

'I'm really sorry, Aunt Alice,' Connie said quickly. 'I didn't mean to make you worry.'

'She *says* she got her nose stuck in a book and didn't hear us calling her,' Uncle Maurice said, in a way that made it clear that, in his opinion, only a fool would believe that.

'Well, thank goodness you're back now!' Aunt Alice looked like she felt relieved enough to believe anything. 'Get in the car and we'll go home and have some lunch.'

It wasn't until after lunch, when her aunt and uncle were both seated at their respective computers again, that Connie finally managed to make her way back to the lake. She called out Ruby's name but there was no response, so she hurried back to the library and climbed inside the window. At first she thought that Ruby wasn't there either but then she heard little fairy sobs.

'Ruby, what's the matter?'

Ruby's muffled voice sounded from behind a row of books. 'It wasn't there. I searched the whole fountain, but it wasn't there.'

Connie frowned. 'Are you sure?'

'I looked everywhere. Oh, Connie,

152

what am I going to do? On Monday
those men will come back and take all
the books away and then I'll be stuck
here for ever.'

Connie felt surprised that the ring
hadn't been in the fountain, but she
was glad now that she had written
down all the other places Eliza had
mentioned.

'Don't worry,' she told Ruby. 'There
are some more places we can look. I'll
go and get my list and I'll meet you
back here in ten minutes. One place is
the bluebell woods.' Connie frowned

suddenly, realizing that looking for a ring in the woods was going to be worse than looking for a needle in a haystack.

But Ruby had already perked up. 'I'll ask the flower fairies to help us. They know those woods better than anyone. I'll ask *them* to search the woods for the ring.'

While Ruby flew off to speak to the flower fairies, Connie went back to her room to find the notepad she had used to jot everything down when she had been talking to Eliza. Connie could remember most of the places Eliza had mentioned without looking at her notes. There was the church in the village where all the ladies in Mrs Fitzpatrick's family had got married. What if that was where the ring had experienced its happiest moment? Then there was the spot where Mrs Fitzpatrick's mother had first met her father—on the platform at the railway station in the village. That must have been a happy moment in the life of the ring, so it was another place they could look.

Connie and Ruby met up outside the library window half an hour later. The flower fairies had agreed to search the woods, which left Connie and Ruby to divide the other tasks between them. Ruby said that she would search the church if Connie looked in the railway station. Ruby reckoned the ring could well be in the church, where the happy women in the family had all stood to take their marriage vows and been given wedding rings to go alongside their ruby one. She didn't think it would be in the train station since rings didn't like noise. 'Where else is there to look?' she asked, straining to read Connie's list.

'At the front gate of Bluebell Hall,' Connie told her. 'We can search there before we go to the village. That's where Mrs Fitzpatrick's great-grandmother was standing when she saw her first grandchild. She was so happy when the carriage drew up and she looked inside and saw the little baby, that she took off the ruby ring and gave it to her daughter right there and then as a thank-you gift.'

155

So Connie and Ruby started by searching the whole area by the front gate of the house. When they couldn't find the ring there, Connie went to ask her aunt if she could go into the village again. She wasn't expecting there to be a problem, but she was wrong. Aunt Alice said that she didn't want Connie walking into the village on her own, that she didn't have time to take her there herself, and that surely Connie could amuse herself around the house until tea time.

'Can't you just sneak off anyway?' Ruby suggested, when she heard what Connie's aunt had said.

Connie frowned. She didn't want to do that, not just in case she was found out and got into trouble, but because she didn't want to worry her aunt again after the worry she had already caused her that morning. She looked down at the rest of her list. 'Why don't you search the church and the railway station? I can search the last two places on the list because they're both here at the house.'

'The ring can't be inside the house.

I've already looked for it there,' Ruby said impatiently.

'I know, but Eliza told me another story about the lady who first owned the ring. She was wearing black because she was still in mourning for her dead sweetheart—the one who'd had the ring made especially for her—when she tripped on her long skirts and fell down the stairs in Bluebell Hall. A young man who was visiting them was in the hallway and he saw her fall and rushed forward to help. She wasn't hurt, but the ring fell off and she couldn't find it anywhere. While the young man was helping her look for it, he noticed a gap in the floorboards. He ordered the servants to lift them up in case the ring had fallen through it, and there it was safe and sound underneath—and very happy to be found, I bet!'

Ruby was frowning as if she thought the story sounded a bit far-fetched. 'Why would the ring fall off unless it was loose, and why would it be loose if it was made especially for her?'

'I don't know. Maybe her fingers had

157

got thinner because she'd stopped eating after her sweetheart died or something. Anyway, we still ought to check to see if it's there.'

'What? Under the floorboards?'

'Yes. And if it's not there, I'll look in the other place Eliza told me about. It's the place where *that* young man— her *second* sweetheart—asked her to marry him. After he found the ring for her, they fell in love and he proposed to her beside the well in the garden. It was meant to be a wishing well so he made a wish that she would say yes— and she did!'

'These stories just get soppier and soppier,' Ruby complained. 'Anyway, there isn't a well in the garden.'

'There's the remains of one just behind the house. I found it when I first came here. I showed it to Uncle Maurice and he said there must have been a well there once that had been filled in.'

'I still don't think the ring is going to be under the floorboards or down a well,' Ruby said stubbornly. 'It would be too difficult for anyone to find it.'

'Well, maybe it doesn't want to be found!'

'Oh, it wants to be found all right! Rings like to show off— especially ruby ones—and they can't do that if there's nobody to show off *to*, can they?' Ruby frowned. '*I* still reckon it's in the church. Rings like churches. That's where they get to be the centre of attention at people's weddings.' And before Connie could reply, Ruby had flown off towards the church in the village.

Connie returned to the main house and lifted up all the rugs in the hallway to check the floorboards for gaps. She couldn't find one anywhere. All she found was a wobbly board across the far side of the hall from the stairs. She prised it up at its loose end and peered underneath, but it was so dark that she couldn't see anything. She went to get a torch and came back to look again, but there was nothing underneath except dust. This probably wasn't the right floorboard, she thought, as she carefully put it back. To look properly she would have to take them all up,

159

and Ruby was right—that was impossible.

She decided to go and search at the site of the old well instead. She found the spot easily enough. Some of the stones that had formed the upper part of the well still made a rough circle on the ground, even though the main part had been filled in long ago and grass now grew over the top of it. She spent a long time carefully searching the ground near where the well had been, but she couldn't find any sign of Mrs Fitzpatrick's ring.

Feeling discouraged, she went back to the library to see if Ruby had returned. She waited for her there until six o'clock, then went back to the flat to have tea with her aunt and uncle.

After a strange meal of peanut-butter sandwiches and chocolate (because that was what they all fancied to eat), Connie returned to the library and found Ruby flying round and round the room in an agitated state. The fairy stopped abruptly when she saw Connie.

'Did you find it?' they both asked

each other at once.

'No,' Connie answered first. 'I was hoping *you* had.'

Ruby shook her head. She looked exhausted. 'I looked in front of the altar and in all the pews and everywhere else in the church. Then I went to search in the station. I even flew down on to the railway tracks in case the ring had got kicked off the platform, but it wasn't anywhere.'

'What about the flower fairies?' Connie asked anxiously. 'Have you heard back from them?'

'No, but they might not have finished searching the woods yet. They said it would take them the whole day.'

Connie wondered if she should suggest that they start making some alternative plans for Ruby's future, just in case the flower fairies couldn't find the ring either. She wanted to let Ruby know that she could always come and live with her if she couldn't go back to fairyland.

'The flower fairies will find it,' Ruby was repeating over and over, as if she were desperately trying to convince herself. 'There must be a spot in the woods where it had its happiest moment . . .'

Connie decided it was probably best not to mention any other plans just yet. 'I can fetch you some chocolate, if you like,' she offered, thinking that might help calm Ruby down.

'I'm not hungry,' Ruby replied miserably. 'Anyway, I can have all the chocolate I want if I end up being stuck in your world, can't I?' She took herself off to the top shelf and curled up behind the books, and Connie could tell that she was feeling very sorry for herself indeed.

11

When Connie woke up the next
morning, she knew straight away that
the ring must still be missing and that
the flower fairies couldn't have found it
either. If they had, then Ruby had
promised to come and tell her
immediately, even if it meant waking
her up. Connie could see the lake from
her bedroom window and, as she drew
back the curtains, she had an idea.
What if the ring had been in the
fountain after all, but had fallen off
into the water? Maybe if she wore her

163

goggles and put her head under the water and looked, she might find it. Anything was worth a try, wasn't it?

Her aunt came into her room just as she was putting on her swimming costume. 'What are you doing?'

'I thought I'd go for a swim in the lake.'

'Don't be silly, Connie! The water might be dirty and we don't know how deep it is. If you want to swim, you can go to the local swimming pool. We can go there this morning if you like!'

Her aunt, who liked swimming— though not very energetically— wouldn't take no for an answer. Half an hour later Connie found herself in the car with a very enthusiastic Aunt Alice, heading towards the local sports centre, which was a good twenty minutes drive away. Aunt Alice had put on her own swimsuit under her clothes and had promised to come in the pool with her.

After their swim, Aunt Alice remembered that she needed some more things from the supermarket and, as swimming always made her hungry,

she decided they would stop for lunch in the supermarket cafe. By the time they headed back towards Bluebell Hall, it was mid afternoon and Connie was starting to feel very guilty about Ruby who must be thinking Connie deserted her. Then, just as they were about to drive past Mrs Fitzpatrick's nursing home, Aunt Alice remembered that there was something she needed to ask the old lady and she slowed the car to turn into the driveway.

'Do we have to go and see her *now?*' Connie burst out impatiently.

Aunt Alice looked surprised. 'I only want to ask about her book sale. I forgot about that yesterday because I was so worried about *you.* You can pop in and ask her for me, if you like. She's less likely to keep you there talking, than me.'

Connie wasn't so sure that was true, but she agreed anyway. At least this would be a good opportunity to suggest that Mrs Fitzpatrick wrote a letter to her great-niece and sent it to the British Museum library.

'Hello, Connie,' the nurse who

opened the door greeted her. 'Here to see Mrs Fitzpatrick, are you? She's the popular one today. She's already got some visitors.'

Connie followed the nurse through to the lounge where Mrs Fitzpatrick was sitting in a big armchair facing her. Her two visitors—a grey-haired man and a dark-haired woman—had their backs to Connie. The old lady was chattering away, looking much happier than Connie had seen her looking before. And when the female visitor turned round, Connie gasped in surprise—it was Eliza!

Connie was very glad that her aunt wasn't with her as Eliza greeted her like an old friend and asked how she had enjoyed the rest of her day out in London.

'After you left, I looked up Bluebell Hall on the Internet and found out where it was. After that, it didn't take me long to find this nursing home.' She turned to the older man sitting next to her. 'Dad, this is the girl I told you about—the one who came to the library.' She turned back to Connie. 'I

told Dad and we both decided to come and visit.'

'And I'm delighted that they did!' Mrs Fitzpatrick said, beaming. She had her handbag on her lap and she was rummaging about inside it as she talked. 'We've been getting along famously! This has got to be the happiest day I've had in a long while!'

Eliza smiled at the old lady. 'It's a very happy day for me too. I feel like I've known you all my life.'

'This is all down to you, Connie,' said Eliza's father. 'If you hadn't gone to see my daughter, she would never have known that her great-aunt wanted to get in touch.'

'But it's not as if I *told* you that, is it, Connie?' Mrs Fitzpatrick pointed out, still searching among the contents of her bag.

'You didn't have to,' Connie answered swiftly. 'I could just tell.'

Mrs Fitzpatrick shot her an admiring look. 'What a clever little girl you are. But how on earth did you find out that Eliza worked in the British Museum?'

Connie swallowed. What could she

167

say in answer to that?

'Didn't you say that it was something to do with Grandma's cousin?' Eliza prompted her, when Connie stayed silent.

'That's right,' Connie agreed quickly.

But Mrs Fitzpatrick wasn't so easily put off. She was frowning. 'I remember my cousin telling me that you were a librarian, Eliza, but not that you worked in the British Museum. And just because I'm old, that doesn't mean I don't have a perfectly good memory. Ah! Here it is!' She pulled a small red box out of her bag. 'I don't have the ruby ring any more, but I want you to have this, Eliza. It's a very pretty box—your grandmother always loved it. It's red on the outside and gold on the—' The old lady gasped as she flicked open the lid. A gold ring with little red jewels set around one half of it was sitting inside.

Connie knew, even before Mrs Fitzpatrick spoke, what it had to be.

'My ruby ring!' the old lady blurted

out, taking the ring out of its box and turning it over in her hand.

'*This* must be the ring's happiest moment!' Connie said out loud.

'What, dear?' Mrs Fitzpatrick was scarcely looking at her. 'I can't believe I've got it back again . . . I've been looking for it for weeks . . . I'm sure it wasn't here last time I looked . . .' Connie saw that there were tears in her eyes. 'And to think I accused Ella's son . . . Oh, dear. I shall have to write to her . . . But however did it get here? Somebody must have put it here, but who? I just don't understand . . .'

'Is this the ring that Grandma told me all those stories about?' Eliza asked, excitedly. 'Grandma said that every time the ring went missing, it was because the *fairies* had borrowed it and that they always shined it up brightly again before giving it back!'

'It's very shiny now, isn't it?' Connie pointed out, but nobody seemed to be listening to her.

'Try it on, Eliza. It belongs to you, now,' Mrs Fitzpatrick said, handing it to her.

'Oh no. I couldn't possibly—'

'Of course you can. It should have been handed down to you in the first place. It should have been your grandmother's, then your mother's and now it should be yours.'

As Eliza continued to protest that she couldn't accept the ring and her great-aunt refused to take it back again, Connie found that her thoughts were racing. Everything made sense now! The reason they hadn't been able to find the ring before was because they hadn't realized that the happiest moments in the ring's lifetime included those in the *future* as well as in the past. The reuniting of the only two surviving members of its family must have trumped all the other happy moments it had witnessed. Connie couldn't wait to go back and tell Ruby.

Just then, Connie heard the front door opening and her aunt's voice in the hallway. She had forgotten all about Aunt Alice. 'My aunt wants to know when the book sale is going to be,' she said quickly. 'She's thinking of buying some of your books.'

170

That seemed to jog Mrs Fitzpatrick's memory about something else. 'Goodness! I'm forgetting I must phone my lawyer! I have to let him know that I'm having the rest of the books cleared out today rather than Monday. The nephew of one of the residents here offered to buy the whole lot and I told him he could go up to the hall today and collect the books that are still there.'

Connie felt her insides go cold. 'You mean somebody's taking all the books away right now?'

'That's right. It has to happen sometime and I just want to get it over and done with.'

'Mrs Fitzpatrick, I've got to go!' Connie's heart was starting to thump loudly as she hurried towards the door. Eliza and her father stared after her in surprise as she dashed into the hall, where her aunt was still talking to the nurse.

'I thought I'd better pop in and say hello to Mrs Fitzpatrick myself,' Aunt Alice began, but Connie grabbed her arm and pulled her away.

171

'We've got to get back to the house before they take away all the books,' she hissed.

'What do you mean? Who's taking the books?'

'The man Mrs Fitzpatrick's sold them to. But there's something in the library I've got to stop him taking—something that doesn't belong to him!'

Aunt Alice frowned. 'Something of yours, you mean? Something you've left there?'

'It's a special book,' Connie said, hearing her voice rising in desperation as she spoke. 'Come on, Aunt Alice. *Please* hurry!'

12

Although Connie's aunt didn't understand what book her niece was talking about, she recognized that she was genuinely distressed. She followed her out to the car and drove them both back to Bluebell Hall as quickly as she could—which wasn't all that fast because the country road was quite a winding one.

When they arrived, they saw a small white van parked outside. Its back doors were open and, in the back, Connie could see several large cardboard boxes.

Ignoring her aunt's questions, she raced across the driveway and into the house. The front door had been left open and, in the library, she found a man packing up a large box of books. All the shelves in the room were empty now. Aunt Alice was coming through the door behind her and quickly introduced herself to the man, telling him that Connie had left something there. 'What was it, darling? A book of yours, you said? What was it called?'

Connie gulped. She had never looked at the spine of the entry-book to see its title. She started to look around the empty room for Ruby. Perhaps she had escaped back into fairyland already, before the entry-book had been packed away.

Then she heard a familiar voice calling to her from the hallway. Neither of the grown-ups seemed to hear it. The two of them were starting up a conversation about books as Connie left the room.

Out in the hallway, Connie whispered, 'Ruby? Where are you?'

174

'Up here.' Ruby was scowling down at her from the top of the grandfather clock. 'Call yourself a friend? Where were you? I kept waiting for you to come and help me but you never did. And now that man has taken away the entry-book. Even if we find the ring, I can't go home now.' And she burst into tears.

'Ruby, it's all right! Mrs Fitzpatrick just found her ring! It turned up at the nursing home when Eliza went to visit her! Its happiest moment was in the future, not in the past.'

Ruby stopped crying. 'She's *found* the ring? Then that means the fairy queen's punishment spell is broken.'

'I know. The entry-book should let you go back through to fairyland again now. So, we can't waste time arguing. We've got to find it. Do you know which box that man put it in?'

Ruby jumped off the top of the grandfather clock and did a fairy dive towards the door. 'It's in the last box he took out to the van. I marked it with a tooth-bite.'

Luckily, Aunt Alice and the man

175

were still talking—both of them were book lovers so they had plenty to talk about—which left the way clear for Connie and Ruby to search the van.

'Here it is!' Ruby said, pointing to a fairy-sized bite-mark on the lid of one of the cardboard boxes.

'What's the book called?' Connie asked, as she opened the box. She knew that it wouldn't be sparkling since it was resting at the moment and she didn't know how else to recognize it.

'Whatever you want it to be called.'

'Huh?'

'It's a magic book. Just imagine its name and then look for it.'

So Connie tried to think of a really good title for the book— one that would make *her* want to read it if there was nothing better on television —and when she had a title in her head, she began to lift the  books one by one out of the box. The sixth book she picked up felt lighter than the others. She looked at the spine and smiled. It said, *Fairy Treasure.*

'This is it,' she said, just as her aunt and the man whose van it was came outside to find her.

'Connie, what are you doing?'

'I've found it!' Connie said, showing the book to Aunt Alice.

'*Fairy Treasure,*' her aunt read. 'But surely that's one of Mrs Fitzpatrick's books? It looks as if it might be quite old.'

Connie flushed. She wasn't very good at lying. 'Yes, but—'

'Connie, you know you can't take things that don't belong to you,' Aunt Alice said, sternly.

The man came over and took the book from her. He quickly flipped open the front cover and leafed through a few of its pages before grunting, 'It's OK—she can have it if she likes.'

'Are you sure? I mean, we'll pay for it, of course—' Aunt Alice began.

'That's all right.' The man winked at

Connie as he handed it back to her. 'It's nice to meet a youngster who's keen on reading for a change—not like all those telly-addict kids you get nowadays!'

'Thank you!' Connie gasped, rushing back with it towards the house.

Aunt Alice stayed behind to explain, proudly, that Connie had been a telly-addict too when she had first come to stay with them, but that she had obviously benefited from the influence of her bookish aunt and uncle.

'Well,' Connie said to Ruby, when they were both safely back in the empty library. 'I guess you'll want to go home now, won't you, before anything else happens?'

Ruby laughed. 'Yes, but let's leave the book here for now. Nobody will find it over the weekend. I'll go back into fairyland, but I'll come back here tomorrow with a surprise for you.'

'What sort of surprise?'

'Wait and see. Meet me here tomorrow at midnight. Wear something pretty!' And, with that, Ruby flew towards the entry-book, which Connie was still holding in her hand. As Ruby

got nearer the book, it started to sparkle just like it had done the first time Connie had seen it. Then it opened itself in Connie's hand, the middle page began to glow, and it threw out a beam pathway.

'Hold it steady or I'll have a bumpy ride!' Ruby called to her, before darting into the bright-yellow beam, shouting, 'Wheeeeee!' and vanishing completely.

*　　　*　　　*

In the middle of the night, Connie was woken up by something tickling her nose. It was a tiny feather duster.

'Ruby!' she gasped, sitting bolt upright in bed. 'What are you doing here? I thought you said midnight *tomorrow*.'

'I did, but this isn't to do with that. I've come to wake you up for a different reason. Follow me.'

Sleepily, and not understanding what was going on, Connie followed Ruby downstairs and across to the main house.

Ruby led her through the empty library and into the hall. The hall seemed empty too at first and Connie couldn't see why Ruby had taken her there. Then she saw the entry-book lying open on the floor. It was sparkling brightly as if it had just been in use. Then she saw there was somebody—a person, not a fairy—sitting on the stairs.

The figure stood up and Connie shrieked in delight as she saw who it was. 'Emma!'

The two girls ran to each other, hugging and giggling and both asking questions at once. Connie realized that her eyes were damp—she'd never cried

out of happiness before—as Emma grabbed her hands, swinging them and laughing, before hugging her all over again.

Connie noticed that Emma was wearing the fairy necklace she had sent to her and that the teardrop was sparkling brightly. 'It looks beautiful on you!' she gasped.

'I know! It arrived in the post this morning. Its the best birthday present I've ever had! Oh, I've missed you so much, Connie! Did you get my letter?'

'No. I got your postcard.'

'Well, I've sent you a letter as well. It's a really long one. It took me ages to write.'

'Oh Emma,' Connie gulped. 'I've

181

missed you too, but how did you . . . ? I mean, why aren't you in Canada? What are you doing here?'

'I met some book fairies when Mum took me to the library near our new house,' Emma told her. 'I've been friends with them ever since and I told them all about you. They know Ruby. So when Ruby came back to fairyland this afternoon, they went to see her. And that's how Ruby found out where I was. It was her idea to bring me here to see you. I had to pass an interview with the fairy queen and then I had to meet her this afternoon in my library in Canada. She shrunk me down and brought me here through the entry-book.' Emma showed Connie her watch, which was still set at the current time in Western Canada—just after four o'clock in the afternoon. 'I feel a bit like Cinderella. I can only stay for a few minutes, not because my carriage will turn into a pumpkin, but because Mum'll be getting worried about where I am.'

'I still can't believe . . .' Connie broke off. 'Emma, I'm so sorry I said you

were silly when you told me before that fairies were real.'

Emma laughed. 'You *were a* bit of a pain about it. But I've got something I'm sorry about too. You know that book we argued about? Well, Mum found it in with some of her books when we unpacked. I feel terrible for not believing *you* about that.'

'Oh, that doesn't matter,' Connie said. 'So long as we're still friends.'

'Of course we are!'

Connie almost asked if they were still *best* friends, but she decided not to. She decided not even to ask about that other Connie who lived next door. If Emma told her that Connie in Canada was her best friend now, then she'd be too upset to be nice about it. And she wanted to be nice.

Ruby suddenly appeared in the hall. 'It's time to go back now,' she said to Emma.

'Will Emma be able to come and see me this way again?' Connie asked. 'Or can I visit her?'

Ruby shook her head. 'Queen Amethyst only allows one round trip

through the entry-book for any one person. She says that two shrinkings—one to get there and one to get back again—is enough in one lifetime for any human. After tomorrow she's going to take the entry-book back to fairyland with her.'

Connie turned back to Emma. 'So when *will* I see you again?'

'I don't know. We might come back to visit next summer.' Emma's voice sounded shaky.

'Listen, Emma . . .' Connie began slowly. 'I've been thinking . . . I don't want you to be lonely in Canada so . . . so it's OK with me if you make a new best friend there.'

Emma sniffed and rubbed at her eyes. 'Thanks,' she grunted. 'It's OK with me if you make a new best friend here as well.'

They looked at each other. It would have to happen sooner or later. It would have to happen for both of them and they both knew it.

Connie swallowed. 'Is it *really* OK with you?'

Emma asked, 'Is it really OK

with *you*?'

They looked at each other steadily for a few seconds longer, before both blurting out, 'NO!' very loudly, and laughing as they hugged each other.

13

The next morning, Connie received two phone calls.

The first one was from her mother who told her that she had just sent on a letter that had arrived for her. 'It had fairy stickers all over the envelope so I knew it must be from Emma even before I saw the Canadian postmark. Remember how she was always trying to convince you that fairies were real?'

'I remember,' Connie said, smiling.

'But what I'm really phoning for is to ask Aunt Alice if it's all right for us to

186

come and stay for a few days next week. Dad and I have both got time off work.'

'Brilliant!' Connie burst out happily. 'I can't wait to show you everything here!' Well, nearly everything, she thought, as she added, 'Aunt Alice is in the bath at the moment but I'll get her to call you back.'

The second phonecall came while Connie was upstairs getting dressed. Fortunately it was Uncle Maurice who answered it, not Aunt Alice who was still in the bathroom. If it had been Aunt Alice, she would have asked far more questions.

'That was Mrs Fitzpatrick. She wants you to go to tea next Saturday,' her uncle said when Connie came downstairs. 'Her niece or somebody is going to be there.'

'*Great*-niece,' corrected Connie, reaching for some bread to make toast.

'Mmmm . . .' Uncle Maurice was concentrating on walking to the door of the kitchen without spilling his overfull mug of coffee. 'Oh, and she wants you to call in some time this week to tell her more about how you managed to trace somebody called Elijah. Who's he when he's at home?'

'She must've said *Eliza*,' Connie replied, trying to stall for time.

But she needn't have worried. Uncle Maurice was already off on a different train of thought. 'Would've made a very good name for one of my dragons, that—Elijah.'

'How's your book going?' Connie asked quickly.

'I'm still on the last chapter. I hate last chapters! All that tying up of loose ends.'

'Why don't you have a cliffhanger ending?' Connie suggested. 'They do that on television all the time. Then you can leave all your loose ends and everyone will want you to write a sequel.'

But Uncle Maurice's brain had now been totally hijacked by dragons and all he could manage in reply was a distracted grunt.

Aunt Alice passed him on her way downstairs, but instead of joining Connie in the kitchen she went straight

into the living room to phone back Connie's mother. Connie heard her aunt confirm the plans for her parents' visit as she waited for her toast to pop up. Then, just as she was going over to the fridge to get the butter, she heard Aunt Alice start to talk about *her*. 'I think you'll find quite a change—she's quite the little bookworm now! . . . What? . . . Well, no, it's not surprising, I suppose, after spending the summer with us, though I never thought I'd see her so interested in fairies. I always thought she was more of a tomboy, like you!'

Connie's mouth had gone dry. How had her aunt found out about the fairies? Connie had never talked about Ruby and, so far as she knew, her aunt had never been there when Ruby appeared.

'Yes . . . well . . . it's a book I've never heard of,' Aunt Alice continued. *'Fairy Treasures* or something . . . I dare say she'll show it to you when you come next week.'

Connie sighed in relief. Aunt Alice was surprised that she was *reading*

189

about fairies, that was all. She wasn't talking about real ones.

*　　　　*　　　　*

At midnight that night, Connie was fast asleep, fully-dressed, on top of her bed when her alarm clock woke her. She was wearing her cropped stripy trousers and her favourite lilac blouse and she had also put on her sparkly necklace and a sparkly hair band, since she knew how much fairies approved of sparkly things.

As she got up and staggered sleepily across the landing towards the stairs, she didn't hear her aunt and uncle's bedroom door opening.

It was a cloudy night and the moon and the stars weren't giving out much light to see by.

'Ruby?' she whispered, nervously, after she had climbed in through the library window.

Suddenly the room burst into light and a mass of fairy voices chorused, 'SURPRISE!'

Connie gasped as she took in the

bookshelves draped in twinkling fairy lights and the floor totally covered in a shimmering gold confetti. Numerous fairies, all dressed in fancy crêpe or tissue paper dresses were smiling at her. There were even little men fairies dressed in leather trousers and brightly coloured tissue-paper shirts. Queen Amethyst was in the middle of the room and, as the music started up, she began to dance in the air most elegantly with a male fairy whose bright-green hair was standing on end. He proudly kicked up his legs and flapped his wings in time to the music.

Ruby waved and Connie went over to join her, taking care to pick her way round the edge of the room so as not to bump into—or stand on—any of the party guests.

All the fairies who weren't dancing were sitting in little groups on the floor with miniature picnic rugs spread out in front of them. They were unpacking hampers of food and chattering excitedly as they passed round tiny paper plates. Connie saw fairy-sized biscuits  shaped like different letters, little sugar-paper tarts with gold full stops on top, and what looked like tiny cheese-and-pineapple punctuation marks on sticks.

Ruby, Emerald and Sapphire were sitting with a boy fairy with black hair and leather bookmark trousers, who was popping open a tiny bottle of fizzy drink. As Connie sat down beside them, Ruby told her that the bottle contained bubbly dew made by flower fairies.

192

'Do you think I might be able to see *flower* fairies from now on as well as book fairies?' Connie asked.

'I don't see why not,' Ruby replied. 'If you're in the right place in the right mind then you should be able to see any kind of fairy.'

Suddenly, one of the book fairies screamed, and pointed to the window. A human face was pressed up against the glass. Its nose was all squidged, but Connie still recognized those dark, piercing eyes and scary eyebrows.

'Uncle Maurice!' she gasped. 'He must have followed me!'

'Can he see us?' Emerald leapt up and flapped about in the air, looking terrified.

'Uncle Maurice isn't like most other grown-ups,' Connie said quickly. 'He believes in fairies and he writes books about other things grown-ups don't usually believe in like dragons and aliens and stuff.'

'Why does he write about dragons and aliens when he could be writing about *us*?' Sapphire asked, looking genuinely puzzled.

'Let's ask him,' Ruby said. And before anyone could stop her, she had flown to the window and was calling out, 'Hi there, Connie's Uncle Maurice! Why don't you come inside and join the party instead of standing there staring at us like that?'

As Uncle Maurice was welcomed inside by the fairies, all those who had heard what Connie had said, rushed over to tell him that he must write about *them* in future, not about silly things like dragons.

'Here,' said Sapphire, handing Connie a thimble glass of bubbly dew.

All the fairies in the room had thimbles now and the fairy queen had stopped dancing and was holding up her glass to make a toast.

'To Connie!' Queen Amethyst announced. 'A very brave girl who didn't believe in fairies or books until now!'

'TO CONNIE!' everyone shouted, including Uncle Maurice who was now being handed paper and pens to make notes by at least a dozen fairies, all eager to appear in his next book.

194

'I wonder why she said I didn't believe in *books* before,' Connie whispered to Ruby who had flown back over to join her. 'Everyone believes in books—they're all around us!'

'Maybe what she means is that you didn't believe before that books could be really *special*,' Ruby said.

'I never thought a book could take me away to a completely different place, that's for sure,' Connie agreed, looking across at the entry-book, which was still sparkling as it wound down after transporting all the fairies.

'I wish I could take you back to fairyland to live there with me,' Ruby said. 'But I don't suppose you'd want to come, would you?'

Connie smiled and shook her head. 'No, but I'm going to miss you an awful lot.'

'I hope you won't forget about me. Children are always forgetting about fairies when they grow up.'

'Of course I won't forget about you!' Connie promised. 'And if my uncle does write a book about fairies next, I'll ask him if the main character can be called Ruby.' She suddenly frowned. 'Mind you, Uncle Maurice's characters tend to be a bit weird . . . Maybe that's not such a good idea after all . . .'

'Maybe *you* could write a story and put me in it,' Ruby suggested.

Connie laughed. 'No way. I *hate* writing stories.'

'Really?' Ruby waited until Connie was looking in the other direction before flying up and sprinkling a handful of fairy dust over her head. 'We'll see about that,' she chuckled to herself, before whizzing off to enjoy the rest of the party.